Several ladies standing nearby screamed when Scorpio was unmasked. And the Queen looked shocked at first.

"There, you see, unmasked as a conjuror," said Kelley. "Can you not see it by his face?"

"It is as I had once guessed," said Elizabeth, softly. "A handsome countenance. Though, I'll admit, very different than how I had imagined it. I think you told the truth when you said you came from a world far from here."

She spoke more sternly. "Would anyone dare to interrupt *my* festivities, to threaten *my* honored guests?" And the guardsmen retreated, leaving Kelley alone with Elizabeth's wrath.

The answer to the Queen's question seemed to be yes, because at that moment Scorpio saw two tall, black-draped figures cross the room and focus their weapons on him.

Run away! Hide!

SCORPIO RISING

ALEX McDONOUGH

A Byron Preiss Visual Publications, Inc. Book

ACE BOOKS, NEW YORK

This book is an Ace original edition, and has never been
previously published.

SCORPIO RISING

An Ace Book/published by arrangement with
Byron Preiss Visual Publications, Inc.

PRINTING HISTORY
Ace edition/October 1990

ISBN: 0-441-75511-9

Ace Books are published by The Berkley Publishing Group,
200 Madison Avenue, New York, New York 10016.
The name ''Ace'' and the ''A'' logo are trademarks belonging to
Charter Communications, Inc.

PRINTED IN THE UNITED STATES OF AMERICA

10 9 8 7 6 5 4 3 2 1

SCORPIO RISING

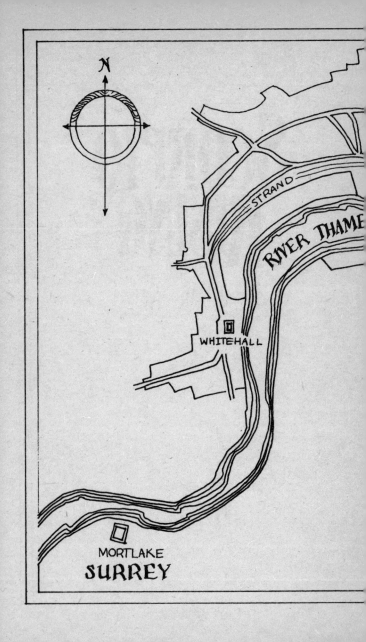

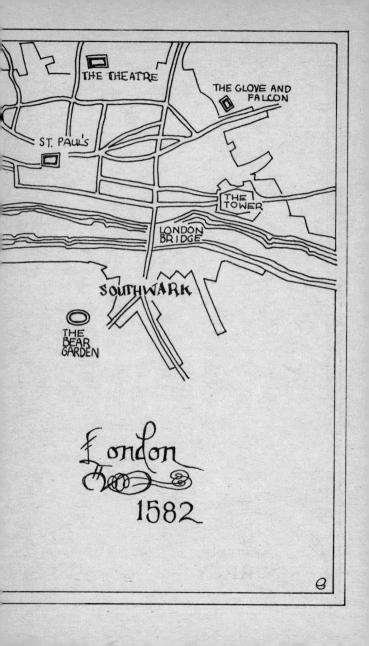

THE THEATRE

THE GLOVE AND
FALCON

ST. PAUL'S

THE
TOWER

LONDON
BRIDGE

SOUTHWARK

THE
BEAR
GARDEN

London
1582

Prologue
Between Worlds

A drift.

I know that I occupy a pocket of warmth and safety where there is no sense of movement or the passage of time. Yet something in me says I'm adrift. A castaway from everything I've known. At times, the all-pervading warmth here makes me dream that I'm an infant in the womb.

Yet I don't think an infant has as many memories as I.

I have no body that I can feel, yet I know the physical part of me is safe, cared for. I can take my identity out, turn it in my hands like a burnished coin.

Leah.

Leah de Bernay.

Daughter of Nathan de Bernay, renowned Jewish physician of Avignon.

Sometimes the memories form pictures: the turreted bridge of St.-Bénézet at morning, crowded with lumbering carts, plodding peasants as unaware as their overworked and bony beasts, aggressive street merchants already beginning to cry their wares in raucous voices. A fine lady and gentleman richly attired but holding perfumed kerchiefs to their noses against the pervasive stench of the close-packed city. Fourteenth-century Avignon was a dirty, sprawling, endlessly fascinating place, with the court of Pope Clement VI as its social center. Famed artists and scientists, as well as ecclesiastics, were drawn by Clement's generosity as a patron.

I'll admit it; I was as blinded as any young girl by the pomp and glitter of the papal court. In my own sheltered, strictly monitored life in the Jewish quarter, I dreamed of what it might be like to live as the courtiers did, freely and with passion. With these stars in my eyes, I was almost seduced by one of the courtiers, Aimeric de la Val d'Ouvèze. He was so different than the boys I knew. They were all boring, serious young men that appealed, no doubt, to Grandmère Zarah, but not to me. I learned in time that Aimeric, like many of the young men of the court, was faithless and trifling. He thought of me only as a possible conquest. I even overheard him say as much to one of his friends. I hated him then, but his handsome roguish face appears before me, and I doubt if I'll ever be able to forget him entirely.

The Plague.

No, I don't want those memories.

Bodies piled up in the streets, and rank smoke from hasty funeral pyres. There was fear in the Jewish quarter then, as rumors were spread that the Jews had poisoned the wells. It was as if they thought placing blame for the Plague would somehow make things better. Grandmère Zarah had often told the story of the goat sent into the wilderness bearing the sins of the Hebrew people—the scapegoat. I understood that story perfectly now.

And my mother went out to nurse a sick friend and never returned. No, I don't want to remember that, but it was important. During the Plague no young man wanted to be apprenticed to a physician. I was the only one who could help my father, and he began to teach me his skills.

Exposed to his knowledge, something happened to my mind. I had been sheltered and lulled into the acquiescence expected of a young woman. Before that time my life had been completely planned. A husband, chosen by my family, of course, and if all went well, children. That was all. Most women thought it was enough, but something snapped, and suddenly I had a thirst, more, a lust for knowledge. I wanted to know about everything in this world and worlds beyond.

I didn't realize how much I'd changed until one day when I joined the women in the public bathhouse. They were a closed circle to me; their lives intertwined because they did the same things, believed the same things. I couldn't imagine my own life conforming to the pattern of theirs, and they seemed to know it, too. I could see in their eyes that they considered me different—possibly even scandalous. That look in their eyes still haunts me. It's as if they wanted to tell me something.

So it was when I encountered the demon in the wood outside the city, I did not run away as others in my place might have done. Ever since I was small, I had heard tales of *shedim*, demons both evil and benevolent, and this certainly seemed to be one of that breed.

When I first saw Scorpio, I was stunned. I stood there paralyzed with fear, trying desperately to convince myself that this was an illusion—only a trick of the hazy light filtering down through branches above. I had almost convinced myself, too, when the thing spoke in an eerie warble, as if someone were trying to sing underwater.

Then I had to admit that it was real. It appeared to have substance; the trees behind it weren't visible through its grayish, vaguely manlike shape.

I wonder now why I didn't run screaming from this apparition. It's one thing to be told as a child that *shedim* exist; quite another to meet one face-to-face in the woods. Yet there was something about Scorpio, something hard to define. His expression seemed to say he was lost, vulnerable, far from his home.

I can hear Scorpio's high-pitched burble of laughter as I think of demons. I remember that I'm not alone in this dream womb. He and I are twins, despite our differences. We're so close here I can feel his presence; sometimes we seem to sense each other's thoughts. He doesn't consider himself a demon, but a person, like myself. He calls the place he comes from Terrapin and talks of it as if it were as real, as substantial as Avignon, his people the Aquay, as mine are the Jews. He said that his people were being murdered by another race, the Hunters, and that an assassin had been sent to kill him. I saw these Hunters and hope never to see them again. I suppose they're no stranger looking than Scorpio at first glance, but they are evil, and he is not. I can't explain it any better than that.

Yes, I know, all this is hard to believe, even for me, and I'm here. Wherever that may be.

He told me he had come to my world by means of an orb, a small, glowing globe. At first when I saw it, I thought it must be a trick, a bladder with a lamp inside, but the steady golden light emanating from it drew my concentration and lulled my fears. I discovered that while the orb was a power, it was one that Scorpio didn't wholly control.

After that first meeting with Scorpio, my life began to unravel, though none of it was his fault. By chance my father was called in to treat a cardinal, Arnaud de Gascon, and in making the diagnosis, let slip the unwise remark "poison." Indeed it had been poison, administered by another cardinal, Bertrand Signac. It hadn't been all that difficult for Signac, in his position of power, to throw the blame onto my father and have him sent to prison.

I can still see my father in that filthy cell. His face was bruised, but he put on a hopeful expression and talked about how I could prove who the real murderer was. Now I think he only meant to keep my hopes up, but I was self-important then, eager to try and prove his innocence, full of plots and plans.

And with Scorpio's help, how we plotted and planned. I can hardly believe now the risks I took. The women would have been even more scandalized had they seen me skulking about Signac's house, hiding in a latrine when the guards came too close.

Scorpio and I finally tricked Signac into confessing his crime to Pope Clement, and I was promised that my father would be freed. I really believed then that all would be well, and my life would return to its normal course. We didn't realize that the Pope coveted the golden orb. He wanted to have it for himself, and a strange being and a young girl didn't seem such a high price to pay. Scorpio and I found ourselves trapped between the Pope's guard and the Hunters, with only one possible escape. We realized it at the same moment and grasped the orb together.

It moved us, somewhat in the way we're journeying now. Although there was no feeling of movement.

We were surprised to find ourselves in Avignon again, though there were details about it that had changed, and I had the impression that time had passed. Thinking to greet my father, I rushed home.

What we hadn't understood was that Clement didn't want the scandal of one cardinal murdering another. Grandmère Zarah would have said he wanted a scapegoat, and my father was perfect. He had been executed.

Ten years ago.

I heard the news when I returned to my home and found it occupied by a former friend of mine. She told me about the death of my father, and some years later, of Grandmère Zarah. It was strange to hear from her lips that she believed Leah de Bernay had been dabbling in sorcery, like her father, and so had been slaughtered by the Pope's men-at-arms. So I was dead, too.

It no longer seemed a great adventure. We humans know what it is to move through time day by day and eventually see all that we have loved and known pass from us. But we were *not* made to take ten years at a leap. Scorpio tried to comfort me, and the orb had a healing touch. Otherwise, I don't think I would have wanted to live.

When I was healed, Scorpio told me he was preparing to journey on. He wanted to find a place and time where the workings of the orb could be explained. Once he gained control of its powers, he hoped to return and save his people. On impulse I asked if I might go with him. There was no one left in this world that I could care about, and though it sounds strange, I felt closer to Scorpio at that moment than to any human being. So we left.

I can't say that this is a long journey, but surely there's plenty of time to wonder if perhaps I made a mistake. Avignon was a place of foul smells, of restrictions, of plots and conspiracies, but no matter what its drawbacks, I knew it. Even though Scorpio's was the only familiar face, it was not a human face. I can't be sure that the motives I give him are true ones because he's still an "other."

But I still have to admit that being between worlds is exciting. Even if I were offered the chance to go back to that circle of women and live my life according to their pattern, I don't know if I could accept. What is scandalous is now second nature.

All that I do know for sure is when the journey is over, when I'm decanted from this womb, I can't go trustingly forth into the world like a newborn babe. I'm no longer easy prey for an amorous stare and a vapid, handsome face. I'll no longer take the word of popes and princes on faith.

I think the journey may be nearing its end. I feel a whirling sensation, a pressure, as if my body were being squeezed over all its surface, blood rushing to fingertips, toes. I feel memory slipping, but I struggle to hang on to it. I must try to take something of my heritage, my identity, my memories into the next world.

Whatever sort of world it may be.

Chapter
1

Dr. John Dee, Astrologer Royal to Her Majesty Queen Elizabeth I, sat at a writing table in his chambers at the Palace of Whitehall. For long moments he stared into space, and then his quill would return to the paper again to make quick, nervous notations. A fire burned in an immense fireplace before him, the heat searing his lined, ascetic face even as drafts of cold air buffeted playfully at vulnerable spots where bony ankles emerged from large, fur-lined slippers. Cold rain occasionally tick-tacked against the mullioned windowpane. When he looked up from his work, he could see the fragmented image of Westminster Abbey. Gothic arches and pointed towers made it seem, for all its bulk, to yearn toward the heavens, though the sky was drear and colorless this November day.

A servant trained in unobtrusiveness had come and gone like a wraith, leaving a tray of victuals, cold fowl, pasties, a goblet of claret. The chamber was large and sparsely furnished, though what furnishings there were had a ponderous ornateness, and hardly a wooden surface was without its carvings of strapwork, cartouches, grotesque birds and animals, the wood polished to a gloss by generations of willing hands. The mantelpiece rose almost to the ceiling, every inch of it embellished until it resembled a fantastic gatehouse or garish Sicilian tomb. And as if this were not

9

decoration enough, here and there the carvings had been accentuated with bright touches of color. The tester bed, almost large enough to become a room in itself, had a headboard of wainscot and hangings of brown velvet and gilt fringe. Firelight glinted off threads of silver and gold worked cleverly into tapestries that softened the walls, an unending display of scenes of the hunt and of battle, rich with symbol and muted color. The room's whole aspect was of a heavy-handed opulence.

At the moment, Dee seemed oblivious to his surroundings, although, in truth, he was merely deep in concentration. There were many benefits that came with his position. Who would have thought that befriending a bastard princess with no claim to the throne and casting her horoscope would lead him to such a high state. He paused, thinking that it had nearly led him to the scaffold in those unsettled times. But he'd had no reason to regret his acts. Not only had the Queen proven herself surprisingly adept at statecraft since she gained the throne, she was loyal as well. Many of those who now held high places in her court had been with her from the beginning.

Still, he grumbled to himself, things were seldom perfect. Elizabeth called him her Merlin, but now, as then, astrology was a suspect science. It went against the doctrine of free will, the fools said, to think the future was foretold by the stars. He sighed hugely. So much ignorance in the world, when there was so much to know, so much joy in the learning.

When he set his quill to dancing over the paper again, he realized that it had dried out and paused to dip it into the inkwell. It would seem that after the honors he had earned as a geographer and mathematician, with his contributions in navigation and optics, the Queen could find a better use for him than playing at a common game of spies!

Even so, he had to admit he had felt a certain sense of

importance earlier that day when he was told that two
"gentlemen" wanted to confer with him. He knew that the
gentlemen in question were Lord Burghley and Sir Francis
Walsingham, two of the Queen's top-ranking advisors with
whom he'd been on intimate terms for some years. He rather
liked William Cecil, Lord Burghley, with his open countenance, lined forehead, and pale eyes which seemed to take
in every detail. Even in the elegant, dark-colored padded
doublet and trunk hose, a huge starched ruff flaring about
his face, Burghley had the mild-mannered air of a very
efficient clerk. As the Queen's Minister of the Treasury, he
had proven his efficiency when his monetary reforms sta-
bilized the country's finances. His political ambitions, however, belied the impression of a humble clerk. He had made
no false steps in his rise to power. Walsingham, on the other
hand, with his heavy-lidded eyes and smoothly trimmed
beard, seemed sleek and complacent, a man who knew
secrets. A staunch Puritan, he had served a lengthy term as
Her Majesty's Minister of Intelligence and had uncovered
more than one popish plot against the realm.

"As you may know, the Duc d'Alençon is in the Netherlands, pursuing his military campaign," said Burghley,
who seldom wasted time on social amenities when there
was a job to be done, "but his representative de Simier is
presently at court."

Dee knew that the seventeen-year-old d'Alençon, brother
of the King of France, was the latest of Elizabeth's "suit-
ors," rather a mismatch for Elizabeth in her forties, though
romance had little to do with it. Throughout her reign the
Virgin Queen had held out the hope of a royal marriage to
the heir of this or that powerful country. To choose among
them would probably have led to factionalism and thus to
war. Never to choose . . . yes, that was what kept the balance
of an uneasy peace. He wondered how a mere woman could
have thought of it, and then decided that perhaps *only* a

woman would have thought of it. It would seem likely that such a game would wear thin after so many years, but that was only the greater tribute to the spell of enchantment Elizabeth could weave about herself when she chose. Something of a magician herself was the Queen, Dee thought with amusement.

Dee nodded, saying nothing. He knew they would get to the meat of it directly.

"When we told him of your occult studies, he was intrigued about your experiments with scrying," said Burghley.

"He wishes, as we had hoped, to attend a séance at your home," Walsingham continued.

"All will be in readiness for him," said Dee. "My assistant, Edward Kelley, is in residence there. He has displayed a genuine talent for reading the future in crystal. *Monsieur le duc* will be amazed."

"I'm sure your assistant has many *talents*," said Walsingham with a cat-licking-cream smile. "His reputation is not exactly spotless."

"We'd be pleased if, during the séance, de Simier was led to give us information about d'Alençon's concerns," said Burghley, getting back to the subject in his direct way.

"I can do no less for my country and my liege," said Dee, politely stifling a yawn. These were duties he'd performed before, many times. He knew his friends were far more interested in whatever secrets he could pry out of his guest than in any demonstration of magic, genuine or not.

"And in turn, we're willing to impart certain information regarding Elizabeth's state of mind that may be passed on to de Simier. Her Majesty is singularly taken with young d'Alençon's charms; this must be made clear. She is eager for this wedding to take place, joining the fates of these two great nations."

"Might it not be beneficial if the marriage were foretold

in the heavens?'' asked Dee dryly. ''I can arrange it.''

There was a pause as Burghley shot a knowing glance at Walsingham. He was recalling a conversation the two men had had earlier over dinner.

''I wish we didn't have to rely on Dee so much,'' Walsingham had said, thrusting his knife toward his plate to spear a last sliver of pheasant. ''The man worries me.''

''He's rendered good service to us in the past,'' replied Burghley. ''And of course he's brilliant. Mathematician, geographer, expert in navigation, astronomy and optics. When he read his preface to *Euclid*, I was told that the hall was so full, people had to stand outside, peering in through doors and windows to hear him.''

''The people gathered not to see a scholar, but a magician. Scientific studies are not the full extent of his learning. He studied under Agrippa and styles himself the Magus of Britain.''

''I know. The Queen calls him her Merlin, but she is taken with pageantry, and I think Dee has a certain flair for the theatrical himself. I don't believe it does any harm.''

''Not if it were all merely show, but you've heard the rumors: that he talks to unnatural beings through the device of a crystal. That he and his assistant went to a graveyard at midnight to resurrect a corpse so that it might speak to them.''

''Pious men know that the world of spirits exists,'' said Burghley.

''I say he takes these notions of spirits too far for his own good. Fear of witches and black magic is widespread. Our own plans could be jeopardized if Dee's experiments bring the wrath of the ignorant down upon him.''

''Come now, you're speaking of an old acquaintance who has been quite useful to us in the past. We can't judge him by the gossip of dullards. They confuse the line between science and superstition.''

"So does John Dee."

His thoughts now returning to the present, Burghley saw that Dee was looking self-satisfied after his jest of controlling the future through his knowledge of astrology. Could he think he had been taken seriously? Burghley could see how someone who dabbled in magic might very well become erratic. Walsingham trusted no one, of course; that was just one of the endearing traits that made him such a good Minister of Intelligence, but it was not Burghley's way to be hasty. As usual, he would bide his time, and watch, and plan.

After further consultation the two men rose to go, their business concluded.

"Have you forwarded my request to Her Majesty for funds to further my research into the spirit world?" he asked, since the time seemed propitious.

"Your petition has been heard and will be dealt with anon," said Burghley in his earnest manner. "You do understand that word of these dealings must be kept secret."

"The times are rife with talk of witchcraft," said Walsingham. "In the common view your studies are suspect. If you continue to work with us, you'll be rewarded in due course. In the meantime I know that your undying devotion to Gloriana will suffice."

Dee smiled, a mere twist of thin lips half hidden in his beard. It was often noted that Gloriana took full advantage of her subjects' devotion, while the lid to the royal coffers remained closed.

A branch of burning wood crackled, awakening Dee from his reverie. How bright the flames were, how hypnotic their silken movement. He stared into the brightness, trying to achieve a trance state and see images instead of random patterns. No visions appeared, and the glare only made his eyes burn and water. If only, he thought, I had psychic talents myself, instead of having to rely on others. My assistant, Edward Kelley, is a true seer, no matter what others say about him. I know that his fits of temper sometimes make him the very devil to deal with, but no one else has given him a chance. They think because he's had a few scrapes with the law his trances couldn't be genuine. But I've been there, and I've talked to . . . I don't know, beings from the world of spirits. Angels. Why shouldn't we try to contact these all-knowing beings? Imagine it, a world where all knowledge, all learning, could be held in common and available on the instant, rapid as a flash of light!

Carried away by his own imaginings, Dee had to rise and pace about the chamber to calm himself. The melancholy comfort of the well-appointed room now weighed more heavily upon him than before. Elizabeth and her ministers, for all their wisdom, contented themselves with prying into the dirty little secrets of princes. When I attempt to unlock the secrets of worlds unseen, Dee grumbled to himself, they say, "Some magics are too dangerous to know." While I search for a route to Cathay, whence ships could return laden with gold and jewels, the monarchs squabble among themselves over their tiny holdings.

For a moment he was angry at his surroundings. All of this finery was merely borrowed. Despite his years of devotion to learning, he had only a pittance he could call his own to pay for his research. If only I could convince the Queen that my dialogues with the spirits are real, he thought, that the angels are good entities and could make of her realm a true Golden Age if we listened to their wisdom. If only . . .

Since there seemed no practical point in continuing this line of thought, he returned at last to his writing table, where a draft had tumbled the papers. Carefully, he began to put them back into order and to occupy his mind with the task at hand. Walsingham, knowing Dee's facility in cryptography, had requested a new system of cyphers for use in espionage.

Dee's studies of the Kabbalah, a book of Jewish mysticism, had led him down some interesting byways. As a mathematician, he found it fascinating, for instance, that every Hebrew letter had numerical value. This gematria seemed to suggest an idea for a code, and he'd been working on it for some time. As he rearranged his papers, his eye noted a Kabbalistic symbol, the tree of life with its ten spheres, or *sephiroth*.

By concentrating on this symbol, one was supposed to ascend from the world of matter through worlds of spirit. He had been using the image as a part of his code, but now he fixed his attention on it wholly, wondering if there was really anything to it. He began to control his breathing. Human breath was composed of fire, air and water and was a potent means of inducing a trance state. By ascending through the spheres, one ultimately reached the crown, the topmost aspect.

As he stared toward the window, the symbol seemed to have left the paper, for the highest sphere now hovered in the air outside and glowed with an inner radiance that was almost blinding. "My stars, it really works!" he gasped, as his vision swam with afterimages that made him imagine the ball of radiance encompassing a human figure. A man. Or was it a woman?

No, impossible, he told himself, realizing that he was not in a trance state, but was wide awake. And he could still see the globe, hovering like a soap bubble outside the window, its contours shivering in the wind.

Getting off his stool so rapidly it fell behind him, he leapt to the window just in time to see the luminous object drift past the window and down into the courtyard beneath. As it touched the earth, there was a blinding flash, and then the light began to fade. Dee watched it go with an aching sense of loss, as if he'd seen one miracle and there would not be another.

But all evidence of his vision hadn't yet disappeared, he realized. Not one, but two humanlike figures stood motionless in the courtyard until the light had dimmed. Like two statues, they stood, as if entranced and unaware of the cold, the drifting streamers of rain. After a moment they began to move sluggishly and to look about themselves in wonder.

"Angels!" thought Dee with excitement. "This time *my* meditations have summoned them!"

Dee burst from his rooms unmindful that he was dressed only in the loose garment he affected in private moments and his wife called his wizard's robes. His slippers flopping with every step, he began to run through the palace toward the courtyard.

Chapter
2

*L*eah hugged her arms about her body as cold rain lashed her. She had almost forgotten what cold was like, but the rain was an effective reminder. The memories of the orb voyage were fading fast. Soon she would remember nothing of being between worlds.

She and Scorpio huddled close together and looked around bemusedly. The sky looked the same, what they could see of it. The walls of an immense stone structure surrounded them, but of course they had no way of telling what it was built for. Certainly, it was larger than any individual's home needed to be. The many-paned windows, some shining gold where lamps were lit behind them, made the place glitter like a fairy palace. Glass had been a rarity in her world, and never had she seen it used so lavishly. The elegance and beauty impressed her, until she remembered that Clement's gorgeous palace in Avignon had only masked the treachery which sent good men to their deaths for no reason. But this was another world entirely, she told herself. Maybe it would be better.

Before they could become acclimated to this new place, they heard footsteps and turned to see an apparition hurtling toward them. It appeared to be a madman in frowsy robes of rusty black, disheveled hair and beard, and slippers that flapped at every step. Before Leah could attempt to address

19

him and ask where they might be, he had prostrated himself before them on the wet stones.

Scorpio and Leah exchanged looks of puzzlement as the man groveled before them. Leah was beginning to know Scorpio well enough to know how he reacted to new experiences: with utter panic. She saw his eyes bulge and the muscles of his face tense, as if every fiber of his being urged, *Run away! Hide!*

The man lying before them was speaking incoherently. "Welcome Uriel! Welcome Soror Mystica! I, too, am a seeker after truth, a student of the crystal, seeker of light!" If he was out of his mind, he was crazy with joy, Leah thought. Then she realized that he wasn't speaking French and that she could understand most of his individual words, if not his meaning.

"I have long awaited this meeting," he said, rising to brush at the muck on his garment, as if he had just now remembered his dignity. "I did not think it would come so soon."

"He has been waiting for us?" questioned Scorpio in a whisper only Leah could hear. "How did he know we were coming when *we* didn't know?"

"I am Dr. John Dee, Astrologer and Magus to Her Majesty Elizabeth I."

Leah understood his words and recognized the language as English. Scorpio seemed frozen with fear. Leah opened her mouth, closed it again and then spoke.

"This is Scorpio of the Aquay and I'm his companion, Leah. Please, sir, may we go inside? Your climate is most intemperate." Amazingly the English equivalents of her thoughts formed themselves in her mouth. The sound of it was alien to her as the words emerged, but the man seemed to notice nothing amiss.

"Of course. What am I thinking? Angels decide to visit

the planet and I keep them standing out in a drafty court-yard.''

This was all very mysterious. Then Leah remembered that she had understood Scorpio, too, when he first appeared to her in Avignon. She recalled that the orb had seemed to take away her pain when she grieved for her lost family, and reasoned that the orb must have prepared them for this destination. Of course, this was a different world, and many concepts were new to her; occasionally, Dee's words were only a blur of sound. After she was exposed to the concepts, Leah supposed, the words would again make sense. She eyed the disheveled figure that led them toward a huge carven door and wondered whether it was a good idea to be entering an unknown dwelling with a madman as guide. But a welcome after their long journey was more than they had expected, and they followed willingly.

Leah got a clear impression of elegance as they were led through one room and into another. Heavy furniture carved with bizarre patterns. Candelabra of glass reflecting a blaze of candle flame. She marveled to see a vast, open staircase with carven banisters; most of the staircases in the dwellings she had known in Avignon were spiral and enclosed.

Dee caught the look of awe on her face. ''Don't they have stairs in the celestial realms—'' he began, and then remembered how they had come here. Of course, those who flew rarely had need for stairs.

Dee shoved the two of them into a curtained alcove when a servant with a tray crossed the room. ''Quick, you mustn't be seen.''

''Do you think it's possible that he knew we were coming?'' asked Scorpio, finding a voice at last.

''I'm afraid our guide may not be sound of mind,'' Leah said gently. ''Keep your hood close around your face. It would probably be best if you did not speak; he had a wild-eyed look when he first saw you, and the sound of your voice might make him abandon us altogether. Right now we need him, lunatic or not."

Dee had been careful that no prying servant would see the two strangers he conducted to his chambers; there was a great deal to do, and he wanted to keep this discovery strictly to himself, at least for a time. Here in the palace, where rumor was second nature, he had little chance of keeping secrets.

Only when he had them safely in his own rooms did Dee breathe deeply again. The two slight figures made for the fire immediately. "The celestial plane has a climate warmer than that of our Isles, I take it," he said, though it shook him a little that angels should seem to cling to the baser comforts.

Still, at least one of them was like nothing that had ever been seen before on this earth. There was something frightening in the wide, bulging eyes above a beaklike protuberance. A monkish robe hid the rest of the creature from view, possibly for the best. The being held in one hand a strange sphere that seemed to radiate its own light. Dee tried not to stare at the sphere, but it drew the eye. Possibly a symbol of power, he thought.

The other looked for all the world like a human woman, with an intelligent brown-eyed face and a shining fall of dark hair that she fluffed dry before the fire. Although, Dee realized, for all he knew, the form these visitors took could be one of their own choosing. Even as he observed her slight, womanly shape limned in damp clothing, he imagined the outlines moving . . . twisting . . . becoming something altogether different.

That made him uncomfortable, so he began to question his visitors again, switching languages, a kind of test. He asked Leah, "Have you come a long way?"

"It feels like we've come a very long way," said Leah,

smiling and looking toward Scorpio, as if for his approval. Her studies with her father had made Latin familiar to her. There was not the same discomfort she felt in speaking a language she didn't think she knew. When he switched over to Greek a few sentences later, she followed him easily.

There was no question, Dee told himself. Only angels could speak all languages at will. He went to his writing table and brought over the page he had been meditating on. "You might wish to know how you were summoned," he said.

Although the female star-dweller glanced at it with interest, she immediately handed it to Scorpio. Evidently, the ugly one was of superior rank. Perhaps the one that looked like a woman was only a celestial interpreter.

"I was meditating upon the topmost *sephirot,* the *kether.*"

"Yes, the crown," said Leah. "That's from the Kabbalah. A book written by my people."

"Your people? The angels? Oh, I see, you mean the book was divinely inspired. I've often thought so."

Leah gave him a puzzled look but held her tongue.

"When my mind was fully engaged with the idea of perfection, your craft appeared outside my window. I called you, and you arrived."

This disclosure seemed to excite Scorpio, but Leah motioned for him to remain silent. Dee was certainly learned if he knew the Kabbalah, and with his hair and beard smoothed and the mad light of joy somewhat tempered in his eyes, he didn't seem quite so much like a madman as he first had. But Leah was still suspicious.

"Yes, we have arrived, but, er, astral travel is somewhat disorienting and I am not quite sure where or when we are," said Leah.

"This is England, of course, the realm of Her Royal Highness Elizabeth I, and the year is one thousand five hundred and eighty-two in the year of our Lord.'' Dee now spoke directly to Scorpio, inclining his head deferentially and mouthing the words in slow motion.

Leah was silent. She had already lost a great deal, but it shook her a little to have her own world and all she'd known relegated so certainly to the dusty past.

''Who is King of France?''

''Henry III is King of France.''

''Does the Pope still rule?'' she asked, knowing that though Clement would be dead by now, a successor, no doubt, followed in his corrupt footsteps.

''Not in England, my lady,'' Dee said frostily.

''Thanks be for that,'' said Leah. ''We've had enough of tyranny.''

Dee grew even more excited, thinking, My stars, the angels must be Protestants! Her Majesty will be doubly pleased.

''You said Elizabeth I was Queen of your land, but who is King?'' asked Leah.

''Why, there's no King; the Queen is our sole ruler, and a great one she is.''

Leah stood silently, trying to digest this. She saw nothing wrong with a woman becoming a physician, but a woman in charge of an entire kingdom? It awed her. Somehow she wasn't ready for this idea.

''I've heard that you star-dwellers have all knowledge of the past and future,'' said Dee. ''Can you tell me aught?''

''We can but try,'' said Leah nervously.

''I have had a vision,'' said Dee, ''of a world-spanning British Empire based on navigation and exploration. I have seen an armada of commerce: gold, spices, silk, jewels. Did I see this truly?''

''This will come to pass,'' said Leah, smiling behind her hand. The Britain she knew of was a tiny half-island filled with barbarians. To her mind they had as much chance of founding a world empire as men did of . . . walking on the moon. But it didn't seem politic to say so under the circumstances.

"Thank you, thank you," said Dee, bowing so low before Scorpio that he almost scraped the floor.

It hadn't escaped Leah's notice that Dee couldn't keep his eyes off the glowing orb that Scorpio still held. "I see you have an interest in our device," she said. "Do you have knowledge of such things?"

"Most certainly," said Dee. "We have discs and orbs as a means to divine the future, though ours are of polished crystal and yours seems to be of liquid gold." He tried to get as close as possible to peer at the orb in Scorpio's hand, but his nervousness at the strange appearance of this spirit kept him too far away to get a good look.

"Do you know how it works, then?" asked Leah.

"I understand how it works, but it takes a special talent to use it. As it may be with you. My lord"—again he inclined his head to Scorpio—"is in possession of the device and so he must have the talent to use it. I myself have no aptitude for such things, but my assistant communicates with such as yourselves almost daily. Perhaps you know Madimi, or Medicina?"

Leah pretended to search her memory, then shook her head.

"I'll take you to my home at Mortlake to meet my assistant if you wish. It is a quiet place, where no one will disturb us as we confer."

The ugly one seemed beside himself with excitement, yet he still didn't speak. "We would be delighted to go," said Leah. Dee busied himself with making more notes and left the angels to finish drying themselves by the fire. Now I have proof for Her Majesty, he thought. I can present these creatures at court! What a stir we'll make, especially when they see the beaked one with the glowing sphere. The royal coffers will stand open to me. Perhaps the star-dwellers will even let me examine their celestial crystal. The discoveries I'll make! My wildest dreams were only the beginning!

"He said that he called the orb here, with that diagram," said Scorpio excitedly at the fireside.

"But by the way he looks at the orb, he's never seen such an object in his life," said Leah.

"Since we know nothing of how to control the device, can we be so certain that he did not use it to bring us here? The people in this time may have advanced knowledge."

"And I suppose the folk of Avignon were dullards by comparison," said Leah frostily.

A silence built between them. "I meant no offense," said Scorpio.

"I know you didn't," said Leah with a sigh. "I only meant that we don't know enough of these people as yet to know if they can truly help us. Do you remember how this one acted when we first landed? He also called us angels."

"What are angels? Is that something like your *shedim*?"

"Yes. No. In truth, they are opposites. Angels are creatures of goodness and light. Demons are wicked, contentious creatures." She said this last with a direct look at Scorpio.

"Those are only words to describe what you do not understand," he said.

"I'm too weary to argue theology with you now."

"Perhaps the orb has brought me to the very man who can teach me its secrets," continued Scorpio, as if Leah had not spoken at all. "If I don't trust him, I may never find out."

"We should be cautious in our dealings with him, but I don't see anything wrong with accompanying him to his house, for our own purposes. We'll be safe there while we learn more about this time we've traveled to. It does seem . . . somewhat advanced," she added grudgingly, thinking about developments in architecture and about a queen who sat by herself on the throne of a kingdom. "This must be a kind and gentle time, indeed, if a woman can rule," she observed.

Seeing the tray of victuals the servant had left, Leah remembered how hungry she was. Dee idly reached over to it for a drumstick and proceeded to chew away noisily. When he saw her watching, he only continued eating until he chewed the fowl down to the bones and then devoured the pasties until only a few crumbs remained.

Manners have certainly gone out of style in this age, Leah thought. Here we are starving, and he doesn't even offer us a bite.

As it grew late, Scorpio and Leah leaned together sleepily, on a bench before the fire, exhaustion making them forget their quarrels. Scorpio felt hopeful for the first time since he left his own world. Leah mistrusts the man, he thought, but even though he did stare at my differentness, he didn't seem so alarmed as others have. It seemed he *expected* me to be different in some way. And he said his assistant often talked to beings such as myself. Think of it, beings like me! I've almost forgotten what it's like to look into a face that isn't alien.

He felt Leah breathing deeply beside him. She was almost asleep. Responsibility for her hung heavy on his mind. He wished, for her sake, that she had never gotten involved in his search, but he had to admit it would have been a lonely journey without her. This was still her world, and the chances were that somewhere in their travels she would find a suitable place to make a home, and if all went well, he would be going back to Terrapin.

Soon, he hoped. The anxiety that had built up within him was now dying away. He looked down at the orb, lying in a fold of his robe. It did not look as full and glossy as heretofore, but as if it, too, needed rest. It glowed dully, like light inside a leather bladder, the skin grown dry and flaky. Even its magic grows weary, Scorpio told himself as he secreted the orb in a leather pouch he wore attached to his belt. He heard the *scratch-scratch* of Dee's quill over the paper and then nothing at all. He welcomed sleep, knowing that in his dreams he would go home.

Chapter

3

*L*eah stepped down from the carriage with a great deal of relief. Between the rutted roads and the crude springs of the vehicle, she had had a severe shaking. The leather coverings of the windows had also let in the rain and cold wind. Scorpio was looking frightened again, his wide eyes taking in everything, and she moved closer to reassure him, though she had no idea of how his mind really worked. For all she knew he was repelled by her gestures of friendship.

Dee's home was much humbler than the palace, of course, but she liked it. It sprawled in all directions, Dee evidently having built onto it at various times in various styles. The structure reflected dully in the small stagnant lake alongside it, flanked by a few leafless trees.

"We must make haste," said Dee, putting a hand on each of their backs and pushing them forward. "Jane, my wife, loves company, but I didn't quite know how to announce the two of you, so perhaps it is best if she doesn't know, at least for now."

Leah found the interior of the dwelling neat and tidy, if not elegant, the floor softened with a layer of rushes. "Hmm, what's that good smell?" she asked as a scent of roasting meat wafted through the house.

Dee looked at her curiously. "Why, my wife is preparing dinner. She would be upset if she knew we had guests and she was not allowed to offer them our hospitality. She would never understand when I told her our guests were angels and that they had no need for worldly sustenance.''

"No need for—'' Leah could feel her mouth water, remembering how long it had been since her last meal.

"Come. Quickly, or one of the servants will spy you.'' Dee conducted them to a large room with shelves jutting out from every available wall. Leah caught her breath. On the shelves were more books than she had ever hoped to see in a lifetime. She remembered her father carefully guarding his small hoard of volumes like a treasure. How he would gape to see this array!

"I'm, um, something of a collector,'' said Dee modestly, though he moved among his shelves with a sense of pride. "After Henry VIII declared the country Protestant, I hate to say it but many irreplaceable books in the monasteries were actually burned. I did my best to save what I could.'' He walked along the shelf indicating: "Aristotle, Plato, Agrippa, Paracelsus, Homer, Vergil—near four thousand, the fourth part of which are written books.''

"I don't understand,'' said Leah. "This many books. How could this many books be copied? It would take *armies* of monks and scribes.''

Dee smiled and brought down a volume near at hand. Leah marveled at the small uniform characters.

"I imagine you of the celestial plane don't need printing,'' he said, "since telepathy is no doubt common among you. But it's been a great help in the spread of knowledge among humankind.''

"Then this is not done by the human hand?''

"It is done by a machine called a printing press.''

Leah thought about that a moment. It staggered her imagination. Books that were not one of a kind, copied painstakingly by hand. Knowledge that was there for the taking, for *anyone*. It seemed impossible, outrageous.

Scorpio was entranced by two large, prominently displayed spheres. "Those are the globes given to me by Mercator," Dee explained. "They are images of the earth."

"Where are we now?" asked Scorpio. His thin, bubbling voice startled Dee, who had been treating Scorpio like a visiting potentate who didn't speak the language.

But Scorpio's obvious curiosity made Dee bend over a globe and place his finger on a spot. "We are . . . here!"

Leah tried to consider the world as a globe. If that were so, then some people were walking upside down, like flies on a ceiling. She snickered. This was too much for her, so as Scorpio and Dee conferred over the globes, she wandered about the room. On a table she saw an amazing array of toys made of metal: a bird in a gilt cage, a knight on horseback, a long-legged mannikin.

"This is another of my hobbies," said Dee, catching sight of her interest. He hurried over and touched something and the bird began to flap its wings. Leah caught her breath, so real was the effect, but after a moment one of its wings fell off.

"I have a little trouble with that sometimes," said Dee. "Never mind, watch this." The knight on horseback jounced up and down.

"It's wonderful," said Leah. "How can you make them move so? Is it by magic?"

"A kind of magic." Dee beamed. "He's propelled by a clockwork mechanism." He showed her where the toy was wound up and placed it on the table. The little man actually walked, putting one foot before the other with an internal clicking sound, as Leah stared.

"Would you like to take one of them back to the celestial realms?"

"Could I?"

"Of course. I can construct more."

It took Leah some time to decide which toy she wanted.

Finally she chose the mannikin and placed him carefully in the pouch she wore at her belt.

Dee excused himself, leaving them alone. "Imagine it, a room whose walls are lined with knowledge," said Leah. "And toys that move. I'm afraid I've underestimated Dr. Dee. If he's mad, it's a divine madness, and the world would be the better to be infected with it."

"I had the feeling that I came to the right place this time," said Scorpio.

When Dee returned, he brought with him a hulking companion dressed in a doublet of greasy leather, stockings all awry on beefy legs. He had a broad face, a ruddy complexion, and though he combed a tangle of rust-red hair forward to either side of his face, it was immediately apparent that, for whatever reason, he was lacking both ears.

Dee's assistant, Edward Kelley, swaggered into the room, bravado covering a sense of unease. He knew that Dee was often angry with his fits of temper and his scapegrace ways, but his ability as a medium had always kept him his job. Now who were these two interlopers cutting in on his territory? What—one of them a wench! And a comely one at that. But swounds, where did Dee find that other one? That face—ugly as a boggart he was. A freak of nature or—he made a sign to ward off evil—maybe nature had nothing to do with it.

". . . my trusted assistant and a gifted trance medium," Dee was saying, which made Kelley puff out his chest. He looked large enough already, since his doublet, sleeves and trunk hose were stuffed full with bombast. And, as Leah would learn later, so was the wearer himself.

Leah thought that his red-cheeked appearance made him look like a grouse in the mating season. She hadn't enjoyed the look he gave her when he came in. She fancied it was similar to the way she'd drooled over Dee's cold fowl. In the next moment, as her stomach lurched, she wished she hadn't thought of food.

"Our visitors were conducted here by means of a golden crystal," Dee told Kelley. "An orb filled with light."

Kelley looked at the two again. Some sort of cony-catching scheme, he thought, though he had not heard of this one before. He was too smart to believe these two were truly celestial travelers. Scorpio was only a horribly deformed man. But that shape—long, skinny, like an eel. Kelley shuddered. Now that the hood of the robe had fallen back, he saw (and this interested him most) small, irregular holes where the intruder's ears should be. Kelley touched the side of his head without realizing it. Some years ago he'd been put on trial for forgery and had paid the penalty of losing both his ears. It was true that he had done the crime, but he'd done so many worse things for which he'd never been punished that he had a feeling of injustice about this. It did not make him any less attractive to the ladies, he knew, but it made him feel imperfect, all the same.

"I'd certainly like to see this otherworldly crystal—if our visitors are willing," said Kelley to Scorpio.

"I'm afraid the device has lost power because of the long journey," said Scorpio lamely. "Perhaps I will demonstrate it for you later." He didn't trust this man and was glad to keep the orb safely in its pouch. It did interest him to find another being who had no external ears. He had assumed that everyone on this planet had the same ugly swirls of flesh sticking out from the sides of their heads. It seemed to him like a deformity. "I'd be interested in seeing your crystal device," he said.

Dee led them to a small room that abutted the library. It had only one narrow window which let in a shaft of light that fell directly onto a table covered in red silk. With an air of pride, Dee stepped forward to withdraw the silken coverlet. "Here is my magic mirror of cannel coal," said

Dee, "where I have oft contacted the celestial beings." The table was painted in brilliant colors, its sides covered with arcane writing in bright yellow. "Under the feet of the table are seals of wax inscribed with Kabbalistic symbols as protection against evil entities," said Dee. A heavy disc of polished obsidian was placed on another large wax seal on the tabletop. Light from the window fell directly upon it and shimmered mysteriously in its somber depths. Leah had to admit that it was an effective display.

"The angel Uriel instructed me in how to construct the proper setting for my showstone," said Dee. "But I do not know if my assistant is prepared for his tasks." He turned to Kelley.

Kelley knew that according to Dee, magic should only be performed when one was "pure," meaning having abstained from all the pleasurable vices and being clean in body and spirit. Kelley had never abstained from anything in his life, but he had found that regular attempts at hygiene and confident lies usually met with the old stargazer's approval.

"I'm at your lordship's service," he said, seating himself in the sole chair and leaning over the glowing crystal.

Kelley was ambivalent about using the crystal. Although he loved the power over others that he gained when he pretended to go into a trance and prophesy, on many occasions something had happened when he looked directly into the crystal. It was as if he were drawn out of himself, and it scared the hell out of him. Dr. Dee could always find a way to pressure or flatter him into looking into the crystal, and though Dee was always careful to refer to those they contacted as angels, Kelley was not so sure. He had learned to direct his vision toward the tabletop in most cases, rather than into the heart of the crystal; it was safer that way. And anyway, he had so many unsavory secrets in his past that falling into a trance state during which he might confess one of them did not seem a particularly good idea.

By now, Kelley was adept in simulating such a state. After a moment he let his head fall back, eyelids open to show the whites. Polysyllabic sounds began to pour from him, as if he had no control over lips and tongue. To Leah and Scorpio, the noises were pure gibberish.

"He speaks in 'Enochian,' " explained Dee. "But, of course, I don't have to explain that to you. It's your native tongue."

"I, um, understand it well," said Scorpio, pretending to listen carefully. "He is, er, congratulating us on our safe journey."

"And telling us to cooperate with you in every way," added Leah.

At last the charade was over. Kelley began to revive by slow stages, looking about wildly and adding an overdramatic "Where am I?" for good measure.

"They understood you perfectly," said Dee.

"Eh?"

"Every word," said Scorpio. "A very interesting discourse."

Kelley looked at them through narrowed eyes. At that moment a bell rang.

"My wife announces dinner," said Dee.

"Dinner," said Leah in a plaintive echo.

"We would be pleased to join you," said Scorpio. "You see, even though I am obviously of the spirit realm, my traveling companion is like yourselves. And I am also allowed to eat and drink while in my carnal form, although, of course, I do not enjoy it. I go along with it, out of duty." He sighed as if in resignation to the inexplicable customs of mortals.

Leah looked at him sharply. It seemed that Scorpio was learning a great deal from humanity. All the wrong things.

"Of course. Give me a moment to break the news to my wife."

Leah and Scorpio were conducted to the dining hall, where they were treated to the sight of a table laden with all kinds of foods: chickens, rabbit, veal, along with salads and several huge, round loaves of fresh-baked bread. Leah was hungry, but this was ridiculous. There was the little matter of her own dietary taboos, and obviously, everything here hadn't been prepared in what her family would consider a proper way. However, the Jewish religion was nothing if not practical, she thought. One was never expected to actually starve in order to observe dietary laws.

Leah gathered that those at the table made up an extended family, which included some of the Dees' grown children and a few other relatives on either side of the family. There was a great deal of lively conversation and debate. Mistress Dee held forth at the head of the table as if she entertained angels every day of the week (one never knew when married to Dr. Dee). Leah saw her look curiously at Scorpio now and then and wondered how Dee had explained their presence. Scorpio was filling his mouth with roast lamb in sauce with such gusto that Leah had to quietly remind him he wasn't supposed to be enjoying it.

Mistress Dee was a tall, handsome woman, who told them she had once served as a lady of the Privy Chamber. She seemed proud to admit that Elizabeth chose only the most attractive people to attend her. Leah was awed by Mistress Dee's gown of saffron satin, the sleeves encrusted with brightly colored stones. The skirt was immense and by some means made to stand away from her hips. The chair she sat in had no arms, which was a lucky thing or the wide skirt would not have been accommodated. The collar was of several layers of stiff material, plaited to stand out in a wheel-like effect. The fashion made Mistress Dee seem a figure larger than life.

"Your ladyship," said Edward Kelley as he took his place, making a low bow, as if he imagined himself cutting a dashing figure.

Mistress Dee looked at him as if she had seen a toad or other loathsome reptile, then coolly continued her conversation.

Mistress Dee's fine attire made Leah uncomfortable about her own garb. The gown she was wearing was one of her favorites, but travel and rough usage had left it a wrinkled and faded mess. Before long, however, the camaraderie and lively talk made her lose her self-consciousness about her lack of fine clothes.

"In my country, before I left to travel with Scorpio, there was a great fear of sorcery," said Leah to her host some moments later. "Do your occult studies put you in danger?"

"My quest for knowledge has always been misunderstood," said Dee. "Even in my early days. At Trinity I produced Aristophanes' *Pax*, which included the performance of the *scarabaeus* flying up to Jupiter's palace with a man and his basket of victuals on his back. The ancients had many clever devices, and by dint of my studies and my mechanical skills, I made a beetle such as Aristophanes would have been proud of. The wings went like this"—he moved his hands up and down to simulate flight). "Three stout lads hoisted it with ropes and pulleys, cleverly hid. The audience was astounded, and for months afterward there was a great scandal, and rumors were spread that the machine's rising was done by sorcery!"

Leah noticed that Mistress Dee laughed as loudly as the rest, though it seemed obvious that this story wasn't a new one.

Later the candles had burned down and the tone of the

conversation became more serious. Dee began to talk of his antiquarian studies.

"According to the legend, King Arthur did not really die, but awaited the time until a Welshman should ascend the throne," he said. "The Tudor line fulfills this prophesy, and we all consider the Queen the living embodiment of Arthur in our age." Others at the table offered their assent.

"I've heard all the tales of Arthur dismissed as mythical," said Kelley.

"Nonsense. He is well documented as a historical figure. Why, I know for a fact his carcass is buried at Glastonbury, along with those of many other mighty princes. We also know that Arthur made voyages of conquest, to Iceland, Greenland and to Atlantis—"

"The new lands to the west are most commonly called America," said Kelley. "After their discoverer, Amerigo Vespucci."

"This effrontery is uncalled-for at my table, sir," said Mistress Dee sharply.

"Arthur made many voyages and sent colonies thither," continued Dee, "thus establishing his jurisdiction. Through these same conquests, Elizabeth has the right to much of Atlantis, and since other Christian princes do now make conquests upon the heathen people, we must do so as well. History demands it of us. The Queen was very receptive to the documents I presented her proving her right to claim the new lands."

The snubs by Mistress Dee having penetrated even his thick hide, Kelley fell silent and glanced surreptitiously at Leah and Scorpio. *If these interlopers are presented at court as celestial travelers, we're likely to be accused of sorcery again,* he thought. *And the penalty for that is the stake.* He touched the side of his head again, without knowing it. *Dee has led a sheltered life, him with his wife from the palace with her lah-de-dah airs. She is a beauty, though. And for* all her rough talk, I think she could fancy me a little.

Scorpio probably lied about having a powerful crystal; I haven't seen it yet. Maybe I ought to slip into the freak's room in the night and *gkkk*—he made a twisting motion with his hands beneath the tabletop. That would solve the problem. I can think of a better fate for the other one. He snickered to himself. She's a pretty little thing.

But if I go along with Dee, maybe the blame will fall upon him alone. I'm just his humble assistant following orders. If he's locked up in the Tower, that leaves me free to become a famous medium in my own right.

Or if it turns out that Dee is covered with glory, I can always claim it was due to my psychic powers. And after we're all a great success at court, maybe I'll seduce the wench, convince her to run off with me. Too bad I don't have time to pursue it further tonight, but I've got an appointment with de Simier's houseman. A small gift should loosen his tongue about his master. I don't need much, just a few bits of information for use in the séance. The duke will be amazed when I read his mind. A lucky thing people are so stupid. I wouldn't be able to make my way otherwise.

Chapter 4

*A*fter the meal was over, Mistress Dee showed Leah and Scorpio their accommodations for the night: two large, adjoining rooms, each with its own fireplace and lavishly appointed bed. There were no corridors; each room opened onto the next. Leah didn't worry about privacy when she saw that the bed was almost a small, separate bedroom within a bedroom, hangings of heavy golden damask screening it on all sides. Mistress Dee swept the hangings back so Leah could see the richly embroidered coverlet over a thick mattress and plump pillows. It looked inviting to Leah, who was exhausted.

Before leaving, Mistress Dee said, "I could not help seeing that you came without baggage. I wonder if you would like a few things to wear."

"I would appreciate it," said Leah, who thought coming without baggage was something of an understatement, under the circumstances. Mistress Dee led the way to her own chambers and knelt before a trunk. "My sister was about your size. She died last year of the ague."

"I'm sorry."

"Do you want to try this on?" Mistress Dee held out a gown of yellow silk with embroidered flowers of all colors.

"Yes, it's beautiful."

The garments were all quite mysterious, but Mistress Dee explained everything patiently. There were wooden busks to shape the bodice, a partlet to cover neck and shoulders, petticoats, and the farthingale, a skirt with hoops of cane in a cone shape to make it stand out. Leah turned this way and that, admiring how the skirt bloomed around her like the petals of a tulip.

"The farthingale is the latest in fashion. You should see the skirts of those at court, every woman vying to have a grander skirt than the other until they can hardly walk through a room side by side without upsetting the furniture. Of course, Her Majesty must always have the grandest of all. It goes very hard with a lady who tries to outdo the Queen. I've seen her tear a sleeve right off an offending lady's dress."

This sounded strangely petty to Leah, who had imagined Queen Elizabeth as a wise, stately ruler, but she decided she should say nothing about it to Mistress Dee.

"Now these." Mistress Dee handed her two strange-looking wrinkled tubes. She had to indicate Leah's feet and legs before Leah knew what she was supposed to do with them. The stockings slipped onto Leah's legs easily, showing the contours of calf and thigh. "Oh, they feel—"

"Quite sensuous. Possibly even sinful? You must have come from a backward land not to have knitted stockings, my dear. Wait, you must have garters to hold them up. And don't forget shoon." She brought a pair of yellow leather slippers from the trunk.

To complete the costume, Mistress Dee fastened a small set of ruffs edged with lace around her throat and topped it off with a necklace of amber beads.

"Now you can go about in style," she said. "I'm afraid that no amount of finery will disguise your unfortunate friend. Is his deformity an accident of birth?"

"Uh, yes, I'd say so," said Leah, thinking that Scorpio had definitely been born that way. It was a new shock every time Scorpio's appearance was mentioned; since she had grown so close to him, she no longer found him ugly. At first his body had seemed a skinny travesty of the human shape, but once she realized he wasn't human, she gained perspective. Muscles lay along bones in another, not necessarily displeasing way. He could move more easily and flexibly than most human beings, she'd noticed. "Was Mr. Kelley born with his defect?" she asked.

"You mean the defect of being a great rogue and scoundrel?" said Mistress Dee with a laugh. "Oh, no, he's had a number of years to practice that. Oh, if you mean his lack of ears, he got in a scrape for forgery and—" Here she waggled her fingers and made snipping sounds.

"That seems cruel," said Leah. Penalties had been harsh in her own time. Somehow she thought men could have learned by now not to mutilate each other in the name of justice. Her father had explained that the ancient law of "an eye for an eye" was only meant to be a metaphor for equity, not a spelling out of correct punishment.

Mistress Dee looked surprised that anyone would question the penalty. "I'm aware of a few things our Mr. Kelley has done that would earn him a worse punishment, had he been caught. Lucky is what he is. And lucky I'm not the one who carried out the sentence." She snipped with her fingers again. "I wouldn't have stopped with the gentleman's ears!"

Leah and Mistress Dee laughed heartily together.

"But seriously, my dear, I think you should avoid him as much as you can. I don't know how John puts up with him. I've asked him many a time to let the man go, but he says he can't replace him." She sighed. "I'm proud of my husband's accomplishments, but sometimes he undertakes experiments that aren't prudent. As to the truth of what he told me about you and your friend—"

"What did he tell you?"

"That you materialized from a glowing ball of light and

are emissaries from another world. Well, perhaps, and perhaps not, but we have had a pleasant talk, so I will not question.''

By now Leah was nearly dropping off to sleep where she stood. ''I'll not keep you up any longer,'' said Mistress Dee, rummaging in the trunk again. ''Here's a rail, a nightdress, and a small bottle of scent.'' Leah was to discover that both the men and women of fashion in this age drowned themselves in perfumes and colognes, a variety of scents from floral to musk. The sweet smells were usually used to mask the fact that bathing was an infrequent occurrence for most people. However, Avignon had been no rose garden, so this usually did not bother her.

When Leah returned to her room, she tried to walk quietly, thinking Scorpio must be asleep. But she heard voices, and, going to the half-opened door, she saw Scorpio seated before the fire with Dr. Dee, deep in conversation. Her first impulse was to join them. Scorpio had knowledge of a sort, but he was too desperate to solve the mystery of the orb, and altogether too innocent when it came to dealing with humankind. He needed her protection and guidance whether he would admit it or not. Still, all that she had been shown in Dee's study impressed her greatly. Dee was not a charlatan, as she had first feared, but a wise and learned man. The orb was so incomprehensible it would be a sore test of even Dee's knowledge.

All Scorpio had was the hope of someday returning to his own world with the means of saving his people. Seeing the two of them there, so intent on sharing knowledge, she didn't have the heart to interrupt. Even if Dee eventually disappointed Scorpio, it couldn't hurt to let the being have his hopes a little while longer. Not to mention that weariness, caused by all the new sights and sounds and sensations, was lapping over her like a warm tide. It didn't seem to bother Scorpio that much, but such a leap in time as this was exhausting. She silently closed the door.

She had changed to her nightdress and had just pulled back the bedcurtains and was preparing to test the softness of the thick mattress when a silent-footed chambermaid came through the door. The maid was holding a strange, long-handled device, and without a word of explanation pulled back the bedclothes and thrust the device into the bed, pushing it down toward the foot. Leah almost cried out. She had seen faint wisps of smoke coming from the device and feared that the careless servant was about to set the bed afire.

With a curtsy the maid withdrew, and when Leah slipped into the bed, she felt a comforting warmth. Rope supports beneath the mattress cradled her. This world might have its drawbacks, she thought, but the people in it certainly knew how to sleep.

To Dee, Scorpio's voice sounded like the cool splashing of water in a fountain. He was even named for a sign of the zodiac; to an astrologer, that was certainly portentous. It was not like talking to the spirits through a trance medium, though he had reams of notes taken from scrying sessions with Kelley. He felt that if he could understand even half of what the star-traveler told him, he would have such knowledge as no man had had before.

But it was all so curious. Scorpio was trying to explain about an aqueous race that created farms from grasses and plants that grew in water. Hydro. Ponics. He wondered if this were only a retelling of Plato's "Atlantis." There was another race, the Hunters, red-skinned creatures spawned on the deserts of Scorpio's world, who hated the water and those who lived in it. There had been a conflict, though it was one-sided because of the Aquays' natural lack of aggression. The orb, with its magical powers, was contested by both races. Could this be a metaphor for the war between the Sons of Darkness and the Sons of Light? From the being's tale, it certainly seemed as if Darkness had the upper hand. And as above, so below. Lord knew, there were evils aplenty on the earth.

Scorpio listened attentively to Dr. Dee hold forth on his theories of the occult and the things he'd learned from conversations with angels. He seemed wise and beneficent, quite unlike Pope Clement, who had promised much and delivered little. And he had a magic mirror to communicate with other realms, much like Scorpio's own orb. The assistant, Kelley, had seemed to be shamming with his language of gibberish, but perhaps Kelley wanted the black glass for himself and didn't want its full potency known. "It was your powers of concentration that made the orb appear in this time period," said Scorpio. "Please, I need to know how to control it, so I can return home and save my people from the Hunters."

"But I thought you were in charge of the craft and decided to come at my call," said Dee.

"Quite the opposite," said Scorpio. "I know the orb has great powers because I have seen it work, but I have no control over it."

"This is strange," said Dee. "Great magic without a magus. Well, I'm called the Magus of Britain, among other names. Perhaps it was not just chance that brought you here. Perhaps I can help."

The following afternoon Scorpio, Leah and Dee gathered in the doctor's study. Kelley had gone off on a mysterious errand, and Leah was glad. She had not liked his curiosity about the orb, and after what Mistress Dee had told her, she was not of a mind to trust him.

Scorpio untied the thong that held the pouch to his belt and brought out the orb, laying it on a table before them. The rest and darkness must have renewed its energy, for it glowed against the dark wood of the tabletop with a luster that made them all regard it in awed silence. To Leah, it seemed somehow alive. To Dee, it resembled that acme of the alchemist's art, the philosopher's stone. To Scorpio, it was an enigma, and one which he must soon solve, if he wanted to end his exile.

"Perhaps it's only a matter of mind control," said Dee, putting both hands out over the orb. "Rise . . . Rise!" The orb lay quiescent on the tabletop, though Scorpio thought it pulsed a little with what he almost imagined was a kind of laughter of light.

"I had a vision just before you emanated," said Dee at length. "It may be important. It was Elijah's Chariot of Fire."

"I know of this symbol," said Leah. "The *merkabah*, the Throne of Glory. It's a way of approaching God, not in the usual way, by prayer and patience, but directly, through intuition. My father and—uh, we often conversed with the Kabbalists in Provence."

"What were you thinking just before we transported?" Scorpio asked Leah quietly.

She tried to recall. "I had knowledge of the symbol," she admitted. "It may have crossed my mind by accident."

"The chariot symbol," continued Dee, "has been the subject of much debate among scholars, but its true meaning remains veiled in secrecy. I don't have the knowledge, but I do know one man who may know of it. He is a Jew, a Kabbalist most ancient and secretive."

Mention of Jews made Leah feel suddenly guilty. It was true that no one here had asked her if she was a Jew. Earlier she had almost said, "My father and the rabbi often conversed with the Kabbalists," but something had stopped her.

Dr. Dee had simply assumed that she and Scorpio were otherworldly. She hadn't lied or denied her heritage, but she had the feeling she wouldn't have been welcomed here as a guest if she had announced the fact. Knowing something of the endurance of her people, she wasn't really surprised that there were Jews in this time, but she wanted to know more.

"Tell me, what does it mean, 'a Jew'?" she asked.

"Oh . . . well, a kind of religion," said Dr. Dee, who seemed not to have thought much about the source of his own Kabbalistic learning. "Another reason for men to divide and struggle against each other. The Jews were all expelled from England around 1290, I believe."

"If they were expelled, how can they be here now?"

"There has been a slow influx since that time, and Her Majesty doesn't concern herself overmuch with the way a man worships once the doors of his house are closed. There's an occasional flap; rumors of a conspiracy, and then a few of the more prominent Jews are expelled, which quiets everything down again, and the colony continues to grow."

"But we were talking about the Kabbalist who may know something that will help," said Scorpio.

"Yes, his name is Jacob Auerman, and he carries an untranslated and unpublished text from the Book of Enoch in an amulet he wears around his neck. He has refused to reveal its contents to another living soul. Perhaps it holds the key to your mysterious orb. I've never met him, actually, but I'm sure that if I approached him as a fellow mage, he'd be glad to help us."

"When can we see him?" asked Scorpio.

"I suppose it would be possible to undertake such a journey tomorrow, if you like."

Leah began to feel happy, imagining Jacob Auerman as a kindred spirit. They would have a great deal to discuss, she knew, meeting across the years.

Chapter
5

*T*he horses' hooves clopped on the cobbles as Dee's carriage took them into London's Jewish colony. "There are still walls," she said, though these were of wood and not half so sturdy as the walls in Avignon. "Did your Queen cause the walls to be built?"

"There have always been walls, I believe, ever since the colony was established," said Dr. Dee, "but as to who might have ordered their construction . . ." He spread his hands in a helpless gesture. The gate stood open, and there was no gatekeeper to ask their business or collect a toll. Leah hung in a window, watching the scene pass: closely packed houses of wood along a narrow, winding street. In the ghetto of Avignon, land had not been made available for new building, so living space to accommodate the growth of population had been created in the form of precariously perched third and fourth stories. New building looked similar here, though considering the open gate, Leah was not sure whether it was because the colony hadn't been given leave to expand outward or because tradition was just being followed blindly.

The dress and manner of the people in the streets were familiar to Leah, as if these same people might simply have been picked up in Avignon and set down in London. She saw boys yelling and scrapping on their way to the *yeshiva*, prim housewives carrying baskets with produce and meat they had scrupulously inspected according to ancient law, and two elderly men in sidecurls and fringes conferring sagely on a street corner, as if they endlessly debated some commentary of the Talmud. She had been impatient with Grandmère Zarah when she answered every question with, "It's tradition." Yet, someone adrift in time could appreciate customs that had stayed the same for thousands of years.

Nothing changes here, she thought, and was amazed to think that with her background she could probably create an identity and blend in, despite the fact that she came from one hundred years in the past. For a few moments it was tempting to contemplate such an idea.

At last the carriage drew up before a narrow house of darkly weathered wood that looked as if it creaked and groaned as it jostled for position among all the newer structures around it. A withered serving woman opened the door and looked sharply at the three, her gaze pausing at Scorpio. She gave a faint gasp.

Dee introduced himself and asked to see Jacob Auerman. The woman withdrew, only to return a moment later to say, "He will see you in his study. This way, please."

Auerman's study was not nearly as impressive as Dee's, but the room exuded an atmosphere of great age, with its smells of moldering paper and dust, darkened wood paneling and furniture of ancient design. A collection of human skulls in a glass case had evidently not been cleaned off for some time, if spiderwebs and the remains of desiccated insects were any indication. For that matter, the man himself seemed unimaginably old as he hobbled about the room leaning on a gnarled walking stick. His posture was stooped, and when he looked up, it reminded Leah of a tortoise peering out of a shell. He had the same tight slash of mouth and tiny, squinted eyes.

Auerman peered up at the three of them. He had heard

of John Dee and had read Foxe's depiction of him as the Great Conjuror, but his own idea was that Dee was rather a Great Charlatan, using magic for his own political ends rather than in a pure quest for knowledge. The other one— his eyes were drawn to Scorpio's face, since he could see little else in the enveloping garment, though there was also something frighteningly wrong with the shape of his body— this one gave him a chill. It looked for all the world as if God had made a serpent walk upright again as in elder times. He avoided looking into those hypnotic eyes, and his hand sought the amulet around his neck for comfort. The third one was ordinary enough, a dark-haired young woman in the scandalous garb of the times. A woman should be modest enough to keep her place at home with father or husband, not be traveling about with a court-appointed dabbler and this . . . monster, he thought.

"Good day, Grandfather," said Leah politely in Hebrew. Surprised at Leah's greeting, Auerman answered her and drew her out, to see if she was like the talking birds they'd brought from the New World. They, too, could learn a few phrases, but that did not mean there was a brain in their heads. He discovered that she could speak Hebrew as well as himself, although her syntax was of an antique variety, as if someone had taught her the language from old books.

As Dee began to tell his story about how two angels had appeared to him from a shining craft, Auerman saw Leah lingering near his desk, her eyes on a parchment. She seemed almost to be reading it, though he knew that was impossible, since girls were never taught to read.

He moved it closer to her. "Can you tell me what it says?" he said challengingly.

With horror he listened to her read it aloud and then look up as if for his approval. He considered this outrageous. Studies for women would destroy the social fabric, create freaks who belonged nowhere. He pulled the paper back so quickly it tore. "There, look what you have done," he said. Though she had done nothing, Leah felt humiliated. Dee looked peeved that his story had been interrupted.

"But what is it you want of me?" asked Auerman, wishing the interview were over.

"The *merkabah* symbol may be the key to controlling the shining orb-craft, which resembles a fiery chariot," said Dee, "but we must know more about it. You are the only one who has such knowledge."

"Yes, many have come in quest of my secret," said Auerman, "but you vain, shallow seekers after personal gain always go away again empty-handed. Your tale of angels is ridiculous. You are a credulous dilettante, sir. Not only do you use magic for your own political gain, but in your misguided experiments in the occult you play with fire. I would not be surprised to see you burned."

"But what is the point of wisdom, if not to teach it to others?" asked Leah.

Auerman averted his gaze as if he had not heard her. A woman debating matters with men was simply unthinkable.

"The Kabbalah is not for amateurs. The paths to the Secret Garden are fraught with peril. From the darkness of the mind strange creatures materialize: the *chayot,* vibrating living beings composed of pure energy, and the wheel-shaped *ofanim*. A man can go mad from the visions. Certainly, such studies are not meant to entertain the Queen on an otherwise dull day. I'm afraid I must declare this interview at an end."

Disappointedly, the three turned to go. Upon seeing Dee's crestfallen face, Auerman felt a twinge of remorse. "I understand your thirst for knowledge, Doctor, but you cannot divide your forces between what is right and what is expedient. A true Seeker follows the narrow path and eschews fame and fortune. It can be no other way."

• • •

In the carriage on the dispirited return trip, Leah said, "I'm sure he has the key to our problem. What can we do?"

"We must prove our sincerity," said Scorpio. "I am sure if he knew that my purpose was to save my people from destruction, he would be more willing to help."

"Even if you told him, I doubt you would be believed," said Leah. "His mind seemed closed, except to what is in his dusty old books."

"Perhaps we could bribe him," said Dee.

"We came here empty-handed," said Scorpio. "And even if we had something your kind would consider valuable, it would not help. You heard him say that magic should not be done to gain fame and fortune."

"We could always beg," said Dee ironically. "Or ask to borrow it."

"Or steal it!" added Leah, surprised to hear the words come from her lips. Even if she were so inclined, she realized she would have little idea of how to go about it. If she did know how, she wouldn't hesitate. It seemed unfair. He had heard her speak Hebrew, and rather than embrace her as one of his own, he had simply snapped his tortoise mouth shut and acted as if she didn't exist.

"You don't know how it was on Terrapin when we had to live as fugitives, in our underwater hiding places," said Scorpio. "The children could no longer frolic amid the waterweeds. We dared not laugh or speak or make sudden movements. A living death. My people are still living it, even though I escaped. I dream of the danger sometimes: dark, menacing shapes casting shadows on the water. The fear. I wake up with my heart pounding and tell myself I am safe. But I still feel the fear because I know the Aquay feel it. The Hunters will hound my people until not one remains. It's not even malicious, just their way. I thought

I could do something to help, but now I begin to wonder. It may already be too late.''

''With the orb there is no such thing as too late,'' said Leah. ''We know what wonders it is capable of. We simply have to find a way to use it.''

That night, Leah paced before the glow of embers in her fireplace. Earlier, when she had looked into the next room, she had seen that the bedcurtains were drawn and supposed that Scorpio must be peacefully asleep by now. However, she was too angry to sleep, remembering how Jacob Auerman had rebuffed them. He had had no respect for her scholarly achievements; he acted as if she were some outlander, with strange ways, rather than one of his own. She racked her brain to think of something she could tell him that would make him give up his secret, but she was unable to come up with anything.

The house was silent at this late hour except for the whistle of the wind along the eaves. A noise made her pause to listen. It sounded like stealthy footsteps in the next room. A board creaked and the footsteps stopped. If Scorpio was abroad, why should his steps sound stealthy? She opened the door very slowly and peered into the darkness. The banked fire in Scorpio's hearth gave a faint light, and she could make out a bulky shape moving about the room. Shadow made it look even larger and more threatening, and she had only one thought—Hunters! How did they follow us here? she wondered.

But as she watched, she saw with some relief that the shape was human, at least, and as it crept about the room, searching, she thought she might have an idea of who it was. In fact, it could be only one person in this household. She decided she'd wait and see what his intentions were.

The intruder moved along the side of the bed and at last seemed to find what he was seeking: Scorpio's garment with the pouch still tied to the belt. The thief fumbled and the orb spilled from the pouch to bounce onto the floor in a pool of golden radiance.

As the figure leaned down as if to retrieve it, in the witchlight of the orb Leah recognized Kelley's face. Just who she thought it was. He stood there half crouched, as if entranced by the orb's glow but afraid to grasp it.

While he stood transfixed, Leah walked up behind him and laid a hand on his arm. The effect was startling. The man nearly jumped out of his skin.

"I—you—he—" Kelley got out in a stuttering gasp, but seemed incapable of saying more.

"Don't be alarmed," said Leah. "I was only . . . admiring the way you crept in here so stealthily."

"That thing—that thing that glows. What is it?"

Leah picked up the orb and quickly put it back in its pouch, throwing the room into darkness. Kelley's presence was more threatening now. There was no movement from the bed; Scorpio must still be asleep. She spoke quickly to cover her nervousness.

"There must be an art to stealing. To creep in past all barriers and bear away the treasure. It seems so exciting. It is a talent I've often wished I could cultivate."

Kelley was silent a few moments as if he were trying to figure out whether she was speaking truthfully or just playing with him before turning him in. At last his ego won out. "Well, most of it just comes naturally to me," he said. "Been practicing this particular art since I was a boy. But I know that everybody doesn't have such a talent. There's a place to learn it, if you're really of a mind."

"Could you tell me about it?"

"It's a place run by an old friend of mine, Lord Foistwell by name. I could set you up there, easy. It's a school, kind of. A school for thieves."

Chapter
6

Scorpio was silent as Leah packed her few belongings into a valise Mistress Dee had loaned her, but it was a silence filled with unspoken questions. She tried not to consider how vulnerable she would feel when she was truly on her own in this strange world.

"I'll be back soon, after all," she said finally when the silence had grown too uncomfortable to bear.

"But you haven't told me anything of your plans. Is it because you don't trust me to keep them secret?"

"Of course not," said Leah. She hadn't told Scorpio her plan because if he heard she was going to go among thieves and scoundrels for his sake, he might try to put a stop to it. Or so she told herself. "There may be a means by which I can discover the secret that Jacob Auerman is hiding in his amulet, but this is something I have to do alone."

"But if there is danger—"

"We took risks when we solved the mystery of the cardinal's murder in Avignon, and if you'll remember, I did my share."

"That was different. You were in your own time then. You knew what to expect. You wouldn't be here if it weren't for me, and—"

"I asked to go along."

"On impulse. How could you know what you were leaving behind?"

"I left nothing. Everyone I cared about was dead. Including myself." Leah paused. She had spoken sharply, causing Scorpio to fall silent. "You aren't to blame for that," she continued more gently. "If I belong anywhere, I belong here and now. And you will simply have to trust me."

"I suppose I can do nothing else, for now."

"While I'm gone, keep a wary eye on Edward Kelley. I think it would be a good idea to find a hiding place for the orb. Kelley has been itching to lay hands on it."

Scorpio didn't look any happier, but he seemed resigned, so she took her leave. Mistress Dee and Edward Kelley were waiting downstairs, sitting opposite each other and looking daggers, as if they'd been doing this for some time.

"I hate for you to go so soon," Mistress Dee told Leah.

"I have no wish to leave your hospitality," said Leah, embracing the woman, "but my Master Scorpio has bid me to see and study your city of London and its inhabitants. Looking as he does, he's loath to mingle with folk, so he is sending me."

As a parting gift, Mistress Dee gave Leah a small purse of perfumed leather with a few coins in it.

"I put her in your protection," said Mistress Dee sternly to Kelley, as if insinuating that things would go badly for him if he broke this trust.

"Madam, it is not a duty I take lightly," he said with a clumsy bow. "She is in the best of hands." He smiled at Leah in a proprietary way that made her skin crawl. Despite her earlier bravado, she began to wonder about the wisdom of going off on her own among rogues and scoundrels, but if there had ever been a time to call a halt to her plans, that time had passed.

As the Dees' carriage set off down the road on a cool yet brightly sunlit morning, Leah's mood lightened. The day seemed bursting with a feeling of adventure and discovery.

The only thing that threatened to spoil it was Kelley's presence. He kept trying to catch her eye, so that he could smile fatuously. He obviously thought she was charmed.

"Since we've been given the use of the carriage for the day, I'll be glad to show you a bit of London before we go to Lord Foistwell's school," he said..

Leah was glad of the chance, though she would have chosen other company.

Leah was amazed, as they approached the city, at how the volume of traffic swelled. She had never seen so many carriages, drays, carts and litters all fighting for space in narrow streets that had evidently not been designed for such a crush. Those on foot added to the confusion, but of necessity gave way to the vehicles. Avignon's streets had been narrow, too, she remembered, but only on market day and during the fairs was there such a volume of traffic as this. She noticed stone uprights erected before many of the buildings, and Kelley told her they were there so that the jostling of wheeled vehicles didn't destroy the houses.

Many of the houses had a striking black-and-white appearance. The framework was made of upright timbers strengthened by horizontal and sloping beams, the interstices filled in with lath and plaster. Each story bellied out over the one below it, causing the narrow streets to be gloomy, even by day. There was a great deal of filth and offal splattered on the cobbles, which made her believe that slops were emptied from stories above. A drainage channel of sorts ran down the middle of the roadway. She reminded herself to watch carefully should she have to walk along any of these thoroughfares. She saw a man shoveling dung into a small handcart, and Kelley told her there were several of these "scavengers" hired to clean the streets. Evidently, there were not enough of them to make a great difference.

Shops were often on the street-level floors of the houses

and consisted of a shutter which let down to a counter. Signs hanging above denoted the trade, usually a guild symbol or other pictograph, identifying the shops for those who could not read. Leah noticed that a great many of the same types of businesses would cluster on one street. Kelley told her that it was only sound business. A customer could then look over the wares of a variety of goldsmiths, for example. With many shops to choose from, one wasn't likely to go farther afield to buy. He said that this usage had caused the naming of various streets, such as the Poultry and Grocer's Court.

What struck her most was the variety and quantity of goods for sale. And the merchants and peddlers, not content to let the passersby simply look at the goods, plied their trade by means of their voices. "Mistress, would ye have any fair linen cloth? I will show you the fairest linen cloth in London."

"Hot apple pies and hot mutton pies, fresh herrings, fine potatoes."

"Swepe chimney swepe, mistress, with a hey derry swepe from the bottom to the top."

"Ha' ya any corns on your feet or toes?"

The messages, shouted or sung in a variety of voices from musical to rasping, made the streets echo with an unending cacophony.

At the heart of this city of bustling commerce, Leah discovered, was the River Thames. She was fascinated by its dark expanse, the wharves on which jutted the stark silhouettes of cranes, awaiting the loading and unloading of ships. Small, brightly decorated craft called wherries were everywhere. She saw people on the wharves shouting, "Westward ho" or "Eastward ho", and Kelley explained that considering the condition of the streets, many Londoners preferred to do their journeying by boat, and by their shouts, they hailed a boatman going in the desired direction. He said that some liked to ride the wherries as a diversion.

She thought that sounded exciting, but didn't say so, since the prospect of being alone on a boat with Kelley was not appealing.

The river was spanned by a single bridge, supported by stout arches and enclosed on either side by rows of splendid houses and shops and roofed above. The actual roadway was a narrow one. About midway across, Leah saw a gate-house tower which guarded a drawbridge. Atop this tower was a series of metal spikes, each topped with something round. To her disgust, she saw that they were human heads, in various stages of decomposition, all the way from fresh to shriveled leather and a hank of hair on a skull.

"What's the purpose of those," she said with disgust.

"Why, those are the heads of criminals," Kelley answered as his hand went protectively to where his right ear had been. He didn't seem aware of the gesture. "Displaying the heads is a good object lesson to those considering a life of crime, of course," he said. "Everyone knows that."

Leah did know. In Avignon the authorities had often done something of the same sort; only she had expected more of this time. "Does the Queen know this is done?" she asked.

Kelley laughed. "It's done by her law, so I hardly think she can be ignorant of the process."

"But she's a woman."

Kelley shrugged. "I suppose so. But she's also the Queen." That seemed to settle it for him, though it made Leah uneasy. Taking a person's life was an awful responsibility. She had never thought about it before, but in her own role as a physician, she might be called in on a case where a life hung in the balance. The lives of the women she'd known suddenly seemed terribly safe. No wonder many were content in it.

The carriage rolled on, and they approached an immense structure, built in a series of arches, ornamented with airy turrets, every line so obviously pointing toward the heavens that she half expected it to take flight for all its size. "That's St. Paul's Cathedral," said Kelley. "It was a deal grander than this, but the steeple caught fire and burned some years ago and it was never replaced."

Are we going to attend a service? she thought with a certain amount of alarm, surprised that Kelley should think of such a thing. She wondered what excuse she could give.

As they came nearer, Leah saw that along one wall, boys with catapults were trying their luck at the pigeons that flew about the ancient building. Quite a few people were coming and going from the cathedral, and they didn't seem to have piety on their minds. She was surprised to see that some tradesmen had even set up temporary stalls in the churchyard and were selling their wares. In spite of her shock, she was fascinated by the products on display, because most of them were books and pamphlets. It had been astonishing to see so many books in Dr. Dee's study, but she had accepted that because they were all in the charge of a learned man, but to have knowledge laid out on a counter for any passerby with a few pennies in his pocket—

A wizened little man approached Kelley and Leah. "Would the lady enjoy the ballad of the hanging of the notorious highwayman Tom Howe?" He brandished a sheet of paper.

"The lady would not enjoy hearing that," protested Leah. But the balladeer continued to push the paper at her, until Kelley stepped toward him. Immediately, the little man scuttled away.

She didn't feel insulted for herself, but felt that all the reverence her father had had for the written word was somehow debased by a writing on such a vulgar subject as the hanging of a thief. She wondered if this was what happened when writing and printing became available to all.

As they entered the cathedral, all about them, fashionable gentlemen and bold-eyed courtesans paraded in the latest fashions. Prosperous merchants in long robes trimmed with fur conferred gravely. Young apprentices scuffled, snatching each other's hats. Others exchanged jests and anecdotes.

"I thought you called this a cathedral," said Leah.

Kelley laughed. "Oh, I don't think of St. Paul's as a church," he said. "It's more of a meeting place. It's where half the business deals of the city are made, and if you want a job, just wait at a certain spot and pretty soon a prospective employer will come by to look over the crop. Down on your luck and can't afford to eat? Wait at the tomb of Duke Humphrey and before long an old friend will come by and, seeing you there, will extend an invitation to dine. It's also a shortcut for porters carrying casks of beer and loads of fish and vegetables between Carter Lane and Paternoster Row.

"And in the evening a different sort of enterprise will be going on, if you get my meaning," added Kelley with a wink.

After a time the carriage drove alongside a crumbling stone wall that looked out of place in the modern city. Kelley told her that the Romans had built it centuries ago, and though it hemmed in the city on three sides, London was burgeoning, and new growth was spilling outside the walls. Leah watched it dwindle with distance, feeling a little, herself, like an antiquated object that the events of time were overwhelming.

The carriage driver shouted down that his horses were tiring and that it was time to put an end to the tour. They entered a street even narrower and filthier than any Leah had seen before, and the carriage stopped beneath a sign that bore, in flaking paint, the emblem of the Glove and Falcon.

Kelley helped Leah to alight and escorted her to the alehouse as the carriage, a tenuous link with the respectable world, clopped on down the street and was lost behind a row of houses.

The place was nearly deserted, with only a few men sitting crouched over trestle tables, nursing their drinks. In contrast to the sleek, well-dressed merchants and gentlefolk Leah had seen earlier, these men had a gaunt, hungry look, and their garments were much worn and patched. They looked up, eyes glittering, when Leah entered, but quickly minded their own business again when they saw Kelley. It was strange, she thought; in the Dees' dining hall he was an overbearing oaf, yet on the streets of London and in this dingy tavern he took on a whole new personality, knowledgeable and subtly tinged with menace. She didn't like this personality, either, however.

"Call your master," he said to the tavernkeeper, a cadaverous man with pockmarked cheeks, hardly the sort to promote happy camaraderie.

The tavernkeeper disappeared, and after a few moments another man appeared, small, swarthy and narrow-faced, yet tricked out in the garments of a gentleman of fashion. Lace dripped from his cuffs, and he wore a black narrow-brimmed hat with a pleated crown and a hip-length cloak of yellow leather. The oddest thing about him was that he sucked on an artifact of clay, and smoke poured from his nose and mouth. Leah saw that the bowl of the device was full of tiny live coals.

"This is my great friend Lord Foistwell," said Kelley.

"You must have brought me one fresh from the countryside," said Foist. "The way she stares, I don't think she's ever seen anyone indulging in tobacco before. One of the more useful discoveries of the New World. Hello, my dear. Edward tells me you're interested in learning 'the trade' from an expert."

Leah was overwhelmed for a moment by the smell of the

tobacco lingering on Lord Foist's breath, mingling with the strong musk scent of his perfume.

"Don't let her fool you," said Kelley. "She's a sharp one. She and her partner are running a fine game on Dr. Dee."

"I don't suppose that's so hard to do, is it?" asked Foist. "You've been doing the same thing for years." The two men laughed.

"You'll have to follow my rules here, girl," said Foist. "You'll work in my tavern on your off hours to help pay for your keep, and work till you drop in practice. I claim everything you bring back while you're under my roof, but when you go, you'll take away a skill that'll keep you in clover for the rest of your days. Not such a bad bargain, eh?"

"I do want to learn," said Leah, finding her voice. "And I don't mind working."

"That's my girl," said Kelley. "I've business of my own to tend to, so I'll be going, but I'll be back to check up on you after a few days. Think you can wait till then?" He chucked her under the chin familiarly.

"I think I can," said Leah. "Barely." She forced herself to smile up at him, and he went away, whistling to himself.

Leah was given a plate of bread crusts soaked in broth and shown to a dark, dank attic room, where one of the straw pallets was hers. She got as comfortable as possible, weary from all her travels. In the street below her, London's voices began to die away, and the rumble of rolling wheels grew faint. Somewhere in the street below she heard the voice of a watchman. "Ten o' the clock, look well to your lock, your fire and light, and so good night."

When she slept, she dreamed she was a little girl again in Avignon. It was the eve before the Passover Seder and she and her father were searching the house by candlelight for any trace of leaven, so that it could be burned before the festival began. Of course, they always found some, since Grandmère Zarah hid it, just for this purpose. A meticulous housekeeper, Zarah had always removed all traces of leaven from the house well before Passover, but Leah enjoyed this small ritual. The following day, at the Seder, the tale of how Moses led his people out of slavery in Egypt would be told, in dramatic form, with much festivity, and *matzoh*, unleavened bread, would be eaten, to remind them of the hardships of the long passage. But in her dream, as they searched, Scorpio took the place of her father, and she knew they were looking for the orb, but though they searched carefully in all of Grandmère Zarah's usual hiding places, nothing was found. The dream ended with the sight of Zarah's hands, age-spotted and arthritic, patting out the flat cakes of *matzoh*. Her voice was cold and toneless as she spoke. ''The bread of freedom is a hard bread.''

Chapter
7

*T*he next morning Leah was awakened by a loud knocking on the door. For a moment she didn't remember where she was, or more important, *when* she was. She expected Grandmère Zarah to come into her room to wake her up. What had she been saying? Then she heard muffled curses very near and saw the low-slanted bare beams of her garret bedroom, dust motes dancing in the beams of light through a many-paned window hazed with grime. The three others who shared her room were wriggling and stretching beneath the coverlets of their floor pallets like insects trying to break free of cocoons. Then one by one they all emerged, looking weary and dazed, lank, uncombed hair hanging about their shoulders.

Leah rubbed her eyes, realizing that being at home in Avignon again was only a dream, but that what Zarah had said about the bread of freedom seemed quite true at this moment. She had never been more free, or felt more lonely. Her roommates were girls her age or younger, apprentices in the thieves' school and part-time tavern wenches. Hard lives showed in faces weathered close to the bone and in sharp, darting eyes. They ignored Leah, the stranger among them, as they chaffed each other in rough language.

After a breakfast scarcely better than the supper she'd had the night before, Leah and the other girls were directed to the large storeroom behind the tavern. Several boys waited there, and they made rude comments as the girls entered, some of which were answered in kind.

"None of that now," said Lord Foistwell as he entered the room. The young people immediately grew quiet, sensing an underlying menace in the man. He said everything in a monotone and rarely raised his voice, yet they were deferential to him, always calling him "Lord" Foistwell, at least to his face, though obviously he was not lord of anything, unless it be lord of pickpockets.

"You're here to learn, and you'll do well to keep your eyes open and your mouths shut. It's a good rule on the streets as well. You'll live longer that way. Here are your teachers, Roger and Darby." Leah almost laughed as two ragged and dirty little boys with unkempt manes of tow-colored hair came in to stand beside him. Soot streaked their cheeks and forehead so thickly that she wished for a cloth to wash their faces clean. The tallest of them scarcely reached to Lord Foistwell's waist, and the other kept wiping a runny nose with his sleeve. Teachers indeed, thought Leah. The elder can be no more than eight.

Some of her fellow students hooted aloud their derision at considering as their teachers boys so much younger than they were. "They're too little to even wash their own faces," cried Joan, a tall, rawboned girl with coppery red hair.

Lord Foist turned his cold eyes on her until she looked uncomfortable and fell silent, and then said, "The look of innocence is a great advantage to a thief, and who is more innocent than a little child? Also, a few smears of soot might sometimes keep a mark from identifying you afterward. It's a disguise that's always available. Now shut up and watch this demonstration. When it's at an end, we'll see if you can do as well."

As Leah watched, a man she recognized as the tavern-keeper sauntered across the room. A moment later she saw

Darby, approaching from the opposite direction and moving very quickly. The little boy slammed into the tavernkeeper as if by accident. Hardly had they collided when Roger came at him from behind and, with a movement so deft Leah didn't catch it, used a small knife or razor to cut through the strings holding the man's purse to his belt. This done, he veered away and was gone before the man could discover what was missing. Darby had also taken to his heels, so there was no culprit left to catch.

"There, think you can master that? I'll divide you off into threes and you can practice. Roger and Darby here will watch and give you some pointers."

Leah took the role of feinter on their first try, but it wasn't as easy as it looked to hit a walking target. Her first try missed, and she fell among empty wine casks with a bone-jarring thump. "Come now, try that again," said Roger with the insufferable tone of the expert, as she struggled to rise. Angry, she tried again and hit her target this time, though success only gave her new bruises to add to old. "Well done," proclaimed Roger, and she was even angrier at herself for being pleased by his praise.

"You must have begun your training at a young age to be such a proficient cutpurse," she said.

"I'm a quick study; that's what my mum says. I see a purse and 'snick-snack.'" He held up his knife and made a snipping motion.

"What's that on your thumb? Can I see it?" Leah examined the stiff thimblelike device as he held up his hand. The sharp blade of the knife and this thumb guard made quick work of any purse-fastening.

"They call me a knight of the horn thumb," said Roger.

After a time Lord Foist called the practice to a halt and introduced them to another of their teachers, a large woman with disheveled blond hair and red-rimmed watery blue eyes. She wore a loose, flowing gown of coarse weave, and nothing much beneath, from the way the fabric clung to generous breasts and thighs. Her name was Eleanor Waterby, or Ellie, as she was called. "My mum," said both Roger and Darby.

Leah discovered later that she was a prostitute as well as a free-lance fence and feinter. Ample flesh was here the mark of the harlot, since it was said that the greater the success she had, the more double chins she displayed.

"That's enough of purse-cutting for now," said Lord Foist. "It's obvious you've all got a great deal to learn. Let's do the lightfingers for a while." Roger and Darby grinned. The lightfingers consisted of attempting to lift a stickpin from the clothing of a partner who held a cane. Whenever a touch was felt, the cane was brought down smartly on the student's hand. Leah cradled her aching hand, thinking that if all the drills were so painful, she'd be glad to consider a life of honesty.

After that first day Leah fell into the routine. Practice sessions alternated with serving ale in the tavern.

Not all practice was conducted in the musty tavern storeroom. One day Lord Foist sent Leah out with Ellie and the boys to "spy out" a neighborhood.

"What does he mean, 'spy out'?" asked Leah.

"Lord Foist maintains that a thief's greatest advantage is to know the terrain," Ellie answered. "If you know every possible hiding place, no matter how unlikely, you can disappear when the law gets on your trail. It's also a good idea to know any places where they might try to trap you, like dead-end streets or blind alleys." She stopped to separate Roger and Darby, who were having a noisy argument that was just coming to blows.

"I suppose that makes sense," said Leah.

"And, of course, it's useful to know just what might be

available in the area, and not too well guarded, as well as what sort of people might pass through and what sort of pickings you can expect from them. Oh, there's a great deal to be learned by exploring every nook and cranny of an area.''

Leah took the importance of this activity on faith, though it didn't sound terribly interesting. Not the sort of glamour in this I thought, she told herself.

The neighborhood they chose was one of dilapidated houses and nearly deserted streets. It seemed as though the city's vitality had moved off in other directions, leaving this one corner forgotten. The filth of the streets was even worse here, as if the scavenger carts gave it a wide berth.

When Ellie suggested she explore a dank, stinking alley, she went forward cautiously, hearing noises inside. When she was partway in, she was confronted by a huge, grizzled rat the size of a small cat. The rat held its ground and stared at her as she stood there, trembling. Finally, she was the one to turn and run.

Roger was laughing at her. ''An old King Rat,'' he chuckled. ''Gets 'em every time.''

Leah was distracted by the people of this place. They were scrawny and pale, and only looked at her sidelong as she passed. She saw a half-clad child in a doorway, eyes enormous in a skull-like face, every rib distinct beneath bluish skin. She saw an old woman scavenging for a morsel of food among the debris of the street. When she rushed over to her and put a coin in her hand, the woman only looked at her dumbly, as if she couldn't conceive of anything so bizarre as an act of kindness.

''What did you go and do that for?'' asked Ellie. ''It'll only encourage more begging. Whenever there's a bad year in the countryside, armies of beggars flood into the city.''

''Then there are other neighborhoods like this, other poor people?''

"Common as dirt in London. I suppose where you come from everyone was rich."

Leah was silent. She knew there were poor in Avignon. But she had the feeling the poverty here was worse, possibly because she knew of the great bounty that existed elsewhere. "I thought, perhaps with the growth of business and trade, that there wouldn't be so many places like this."

"The poor are with us always," said Ellie, which seemed as far as she could go toward explaining the problem. Taking a pewter flask from where it nestled in her ample bosom, she took a healthy swig. She offered Leah a swallow, but it was declined.

"I don't know why you brought me here. There can't be anything left to steal."

"There's always something to steal," said Roger matter-of-factly. "Mark of a good thief."

"Even if we don't find anything," said Ellie, "we usually take beginners to places the law doesn't much care about. It's safer that way. You're not ready to take on the Keepers of the Queen's Peace just yet."

Leah sat on a wine keg in the practice room watching Joan attempt to reach into a pocket strung upon a cord. Little bells were fastened to the pocket's top. Inside were some coins, and the thief that could take out a coin without any noise was declared a "public foister." Alongside it was a purse, strung from the same cord. Anyone who could take a piece of silver out of it without ringing the bells was called a "judicial nipper." Joan moved her hand carefully, but the jingle of bells spoiled her attempt and she turned away, smothering a curse. Leah got down from the keg and went to the pocket. Hours of practice and a steady hand allowed her to reach carefully into the pocket. No bells rang. Smiling, she opened her hand and showed the coin.

"Don't gloat, my girl," said Joan. "Practice in a back

room ain't nothing like trying your luck on the streets.''

Leah sighed. ''I begin to think we'll never get a chance to put any of this to use. Perhaps Lord Foist just uses this thieves' school as a blind. All he really wants is unpaid labor in his tavern.'' She was beginning to feel that the cleverness of London thieves was vastly overrated. She had learned to do these things so quickly; there was nothing to it.

Impatient to try her hand in the real world, she asked Ellie when she'd be allowed to do her first job. She would have asked Lord Foist, but his personality was so chillingly forbidding that few students asked him anything.

''Are you sure you're ready?'' asked Ellie. ''You've been here only a fortnight. Hardly long enough to become a seasoned thief.''

''The exercises are so boring, the same thing over and over.''

''True, but considering the penalties if one is caught, it's best to be well practiced.''

Leah remembered that Kelley's ears had been forfeit for his crime of forgery. She had also heard of thieves who'd had their hands lopped off. This was done because everyone knew such a punishment would keep the culprit from stealing again. However, Leah had heard about the punishment from a successful one-handed thief she'd talked to at the Glove and Falcon. Still, Ellie had a point. If failure led to such dire punishment, it would be best to be fully prepared. But she knew she was ready now, so she persevered in asking. After all, she couldn't help Scorpio if she was buried in an alehouse forever.

Several days later Ellie came by as Leah was just getting off duty at the tavern.

''I know you're a stranger to London, dear. Maybe you'd

like to get away a bit, see some sights and have some fun for a change.''

"I'd like that," said Leah, who had the feeling that Ellie was tired of her appeals to be given a chance to show what she had learned and was only finding another way to put her off. "But wouldn't Lord Foistwell object?"

"Oh, no, it's something his lordship would approve of. I can show you how easy the pickin's are where people congregate."

The four of them, Ellie, Leah, Roger and Darby, set out in a festive mood for the Bear Garden. That was what they called it. Leah knew what bears were, and what gardens were, but put them together, and she had no idea what she might see.

Roger and Darby gamboled on ahead of them, children again, their voices raised in some ongoing sibling argument, and Ellie walked quite briskly for her weight. It was a fine day, and Leah was glad to be away from the dirty tavern and the threatening presence of Lord Foistwell.

Whatever the Bear Garden was, it was located on the south bank of the river in an area more or less remote from the city proper. They left the close-clustering behind and walked past open fields where the sweetness of dried grass came as a surprise after the city's stench. In one sense they hadn't escaped the city because as they walked along, others began to join them, until it was obvious they were part of a crowd all moving in one direction. "I told you this is one way a good thief can line his pockets with gold," said Ellie, indicating how Roger and Darby moved like quicksilver among the ambling masses.

Ahead Leah saw a circular structure with a thatched roof upheld by widely spaced pillars. Beside this was a pond between two long sheds, with a smaller shed to one side. As she came nearer, she heard frantic yapping and barking from the long sheds and caught the musky scent of confined animals as the wind turned in her direction.

Leah couldn't help catching something of the holiday mood of this crowd. Brightly colored pennants were strung on the structures, and she could hear music, a shrill piping. "Give way, give way," shouted the people around her, and the crowd opened to admit a parade of sorts. Minstrels in colorful costumes played horns and flutes. Behind them came two men leading an immense, lumbering bear between them on stout chains.

"What bear is it, boys?" asked Ellie, trying to peer between members of the jostling crowd.

"It's Don Jon, Mum," said Roger.

"I see him," said Ellie. "I know him by his torn ear. He's a rare fighter. There'll be a good match today."

Leah began to have misgivings as they approached the arena. They paid their penny and were admitted inside. Seats for the spectators were provided all around the circle. This was roofed over, but the arena itself was open to the sky, probably to provide more light. Before the entertainment began, Leah noticed that many of the spectators were gathered in groups. Money was changing hands, and by the odd snatches of conversation she heard, she understood that odds were being taken on the outcome of whatever contest this was to be. She noticed that the people who gathered ran the spectrum of the social classes, from richly dressed lords and ladies to raggedly clothed apprentices and laborers. The only thing they had in common was the glitter of anticipation in their eyes.

After a time the bearkeepers led their charge into the center of the arena. The chains were fastened to a framework that gave the animal some freedom of movement, or as far as the chains would allow.

"Here come the mastiffs," shouted Darby, jumping up and down on his seat. Leah heard a chorus of yelps, barks, and whines with a counterpoint of harsh, deep-voiced growls as several large dogs were brought in, straining at their leashes.

"But what are we to see?" asked Leah, just as the keepers slipped the leashes and the dogs were set on the great bear.

When the bear stood up, it seemed eight feet tall, but none of the dogs hesitated. Two circled, barking loudly, while three more launched themselves directly at the bear's throat. Sweeps of immense shaggy paws sent dogs flying to left and right. One dog was hit squarely. He cried out in agony and was sent rolling. When he stopped, he tried to rise but fell back. His rib cage on one side looked crushed and a drool of blood descended from his open mouth. Occasionally, a dog would get through the bear's defenses and set his teeth in the hairy hide. Then the bear would shake himself violently to release the dog's hold, and the jaws would shear through hide and flesh, causing a jet of blood.

All the animals seemed half crazed by the blood scent that hung heavy in the air. All the animals, including the watchers, Leah thought, becoming nauseated at the sight. The people were drunk on the spectacle; they seemed to have no notion of the cruelty behind it.

She put a hand on Ellie's shoulder. She had to shake the woman to get her attention. "I've had enough of this," she said. "I'm going. You can stay if you want to."

Blindly, she fought free of the crowd and tried to close her ears to the noises behind her. She felt only a little better when she was outside, since she knew the brutal spectacle continued. After a moment she heard hurried footsteps and turned to see Ellie.

"What's the matter? Did the crowd frighten you?" asked Ellie. "Sometimes the spirit of the bear-baiting gets to them and fights break out among the men. They lay about with swords and daggers, cutting off fingers, ears—"

"Is that what you people do for sport here?" asked Leah.

"Well . . . some do, anyway," said Ellie, puzzled, as if she couldn't understand why anyone would object to such action and fun. "The sport we chiefly have in mind is the good old nip and foist. The noise and excitement are great cover. Roger and Darby are trying their luck now."

"Shall we wait for them?"

"No. They may have to flee quickly, and we'd only be an encumbrance."

Ellie conferred with Lord Foist, and it was decided that Leah should have the opportunity to put her learning to the test. "You'll be our 'stale,'" said Ellie, "our decoy. Try this." To Leah's shock and amazement, Ellie lifted her skirt until her whole calf and a part of her doughy thigh showed. Then she appeared to be refastening her garter. "Believe me, this stops the gentlemen in their tracks. It becomes an easy matter for Roger to creep up behind him. We certainly know where the gentleman's attention is going to be."

"B-but you showed practically your . . . whole leg!" said Leah dumbfoundedly. She was as shocked as if Ellie had calmly discussed disrobing on a street corner.

"It's just a leg, dear. Little enough to ask, that is, if you're really serious about doing a job."

"All right." Leah bit her lip and hoisted her skirt, but she knew she'd feel guilty about it for days afterward.

"It's not really a frivolous thing, after all," said Ellie. "Roger's life depends upon it, you know."

Leah felt a chill, considering this. Ellie was right. When you became an active participant in anything, it seemed the stakes went up.

Roger and Leah strolled along a busy street, appraising the passersby. When Roger spotted a well-dressed gentleman, he poked Leah and pointed him out. They walked nonchalantly past him and then darted down an alley to cut him off at the next street.

Feeling sweaty and disheveled, the very antithesis of what she must appear, Leah positioned herself where the gentleman couldn't miss seeing her as he came by. Men jostled each other on the street. She wouldn't just be displaying herself for their quarry. Everyone would see. She felt mortified. Better just break and run now, before Roger's life was jeopardized by her foolishness. But if I don't do this, I'll be giving up in defeat. I'll never learn what I need to know to get the talisman.

As he approached, Leah saw that the gentleman they'd chosen had a coarse, debauched-looking face. Maybe that was only her imagination. She took a deep breath and, pretending her garter had broken, lifted up her skirt.

She saw the gentleman slow down, pause, stop to stare, a grin smearing itself across his gross features. She froze as he began to approach her. Ellie told her she should smile, try to hold his attention as long as possible, but she felt paralyzed, riveted to the spot.

By this time Roger had come up silently behind the man and had done his part. She saw him wave jauntily in signal that it was time for her to flee as well.

"Hello, missy," began the man, coming very near.

Leah was in a panic. The real situation was so different than practice. She hadn't thought she'd be so scared that she would not be able to move.

As he carelessly put his hand to his hip, he discovered that his purse was gone, and reaching out, he grabbed Leah by the sleeve and began to cry out loudly. "Thieves, robbers! I've got one of 'em. Call the constable!"

Roger came up from one direction, Darby from another, shouting something about "Sister, sister, come home. Our mother's sick!" Roger pulled hard on the lacings that attached Leah's sleeve to the gown and they tore away. Feeling herself freed, Leah began to run. She heard pounding feet behind her, but now panic seemed to be helping her because she ran as she had never run before. Slipping through a gap in the heavy street traffic, she lost any pursuers for good, but even after she holed up in a hiding place discovered on one of her earlier explorations, she couldn't seem to stop shaking. All right, she told herself. This isn't so easy. And all didn't go as planned, but I made it. I'm still here, and all in one piece.

After a time she returned to the Glove and Falcon, sure that she would be in deep disgrace and that it would be a long time before anyone wanted to work with her again. When she arrived, she was in time to overhear Roger telling the other apprentices a riotous version of what had occurred. Her face reddened as the others looked up at her and laughed, but that was the only chastisement she received for her failure. She supposed that the real punishment for a thief's failure could be so severe it was the only threat needed. I'll do better next time, she vowed.

Ellie came into the practice room, walking a little unsteadily. Her breath was heavy with the smell of ale as she spoke to Leah. "I promised to show you a good time in London, and our last outing didn't work out so well. Come along with me and I swear you'll have a good time."

"I can't. I have to go on duty in a few more hours," said Leah, though after the debacle of the bear-baiting, she was glad to have this excuse.

"I guarantee you'll like this. No blood—well, nobody really gets hurt, in any case. And the crowd is almost as good as at the bear-baiting," said Ellie. "Come along. You can't go home from London and tell them you haven't seen a play."

Finally giving in to Ellie's promises, Leah agreed to go. She had overheard people talking excitedly about this new form of entertainment, and she had wanted to see it for herself. It would give her something to tell Scorpio when she got back. She knew she could never explain the bear-baiting to him.

"We'll have a bit of a walk," said Ellie. "Bluenose Puritans believe this sort of entertainment's rude and common. Stodgy old Lord Mayor would ban plays altogether, says the crowds gathering causes disease, and fires could be caused by stage directions like 'chambers shot off within.' So they built the theatre in Shoreditch where the city's writ isn't in force. The Queen thinks it's all right, though, and is always holding masques and plays at court. Good old Queen Bess." Ellie raised her flask in a toast and drank deeply.

After a long trudge, they reached the edge of the city where close-set buildings gave way to open fields. Leah saw a round structure set off to itself. As at the bear-baiting, a crowd had gathered and was streaming in through the entrances, evidently called by the blaring of trumpets and the raising of colorful flags that rippled in the wind. She couldn't help feeling excited. Ellie handed over a few coins to a man at the entrance, and he dropped the money into a box.

Leah found the building curious. There was no roof over the central part, though roofs and awnings covered the tiers of seats and private boxes along the sides where the wealthy folk sat. A square wooden platform extended out into the center. Crowds of the poor folk ebbed and flowed through this section; people ate, visited, joked.

At last another trumpet call sounded, and a group of flamboyantly dressed people trooped onto the platform. "What are they going to do?" asked Leah.

"Just watch."

Leah watched, mesmerized as action and pageantry unfolded before her. The speeches and actions seemed outlandish, yet there was a magic in it. More seasoned playgoers around her shouted their approval or tried to bandy words with the actors. A little later on, Leah screamed as one man seemed to stab another and blood splattered on the stage, sending a few drops out among the groundlings.

"It's real!" she said, turning on Ellie. "The bear-baiting was bad enough, but to watch two men rend each other—"

"It's only a bladder full of blood from the butcher's," said Ellie. "Makes it more realistic. Look, do you think a dead man could twitch like that." A moment later the dead man shouted a curse at a heckler in the audience, so Leah knew he was all right.

Then a little later she whispered to Ellie, "Am I wrong or is that lady . . . a boy?"

"Certainly she's a boy. You don't expect real womenfolk to get up there and disport themselves so shamefully, do you? He does make a pretty wench, though, don't he?"

Leah thought it odd that Ellie, considering her occupation, would talk about a shameful profession, but she was silent, caught up again in action that was obviously false, yet in another way quite real.

Then just when things were getting exciting, Leah felt a hand on her arm and turned to see Joan, from the thieves' school. "Lord Foist sent me to get you. Said you'd take the evening shift in place of your afternoon one or he'd raise hell."

Knowing how effective Lord Foist was at that endeavor, Leah turned reluctantly away. "Will you watch till the end and let me know how it turns out?" she asked Ellie.

Ellie nodded.

Some moments after Leah had gone, there was a sudden, brilliant flash of light on the stage, making Ellie and the other groundlings shield their eyes. Ellie knew about the trapdoor in the middle of the stage by which ghosts and the like were made to appear, but in conjunction with the flashing lights, it looked quite realistic.

Out of the afterimages stepped two figures. They were obviously masked actors in flowing black gowns, but the effect was startling. Their skin was a fearsome red. Each had a bone running lengthwise across his face, creating a beaklike appearance, and spiraling ram's horns to either side of his head. One of them, the taller, slenderer one, carried a small, glowing golden ball.

Ellie struggled to fit this apparition into the plot of the play. It must be some grave portent appearing to the King, she thought, but the King was backpedaling quickly, his crown falling from his head, and the "lady" whom Leah had remarked on was making a speedy exit, skirts flying around long, boyish legs.

Lethor awoke from what he thought was a strange dream, to find himself standing on a crude platform in a primitive building only half roofed, the center open to the sky. He saw that he and his companion, Ardon, were surrounded by a crowd of the species that inhabited this world, as if the Hunters were somehow on display for this ragged, ill-smelling herd. "I wonder what manner of place this is," he said aloud, though he expected no answer from his more burly companion, who was, after all, a Beta, not bred for thinking, though he followed orders well. The orb that he and Ardon held between them reminded him that they had followed Scorpio and the female indigene here because there was a small commitment as yet unfulfilled—Scorpio's death. The hunt had not gone well, Lethor admitted. What should have been simple had been complicated by the orb which Scorpio had stolen. And these native creatures had been involved in the chase, as well. Undisciplined, he thought, this will not do at all. Anxiety made his near-vision cut in, and he was treated to a closer sight of the faces of the groundlings, some pockmarked, some gap-toothed. With an effort, he suppressed this visual reflex.

A Hunter was supposed to feel no emotion toward his prey, but Lethor was finding it increasingly difficult not to feel something approaching anger toward the elusive Aquay.

He had hoped, when they emerged from orb space, to find some clue as to where his quarry had gone. After all, an alien could hardly go unnoticed here.

The crowd, which had been somewhat stunned by the first appearance of the orb-travelers, soon began to stamp their feet and shout for the play to continue. The actors had gathered at the edge of the stage and gesticulated as they talked things over. They appeared to be incensed that they had been driven from the stage. The King brandished his sword and began to approach aggressively, as if his training in the mock combat of the theater gave him confidence. "Ho there, we know you're from a rival company, sent here to spoil the performance."

Lethor experienced the same instant understanding of the creature's language as Leah had earlier, though there were enough alien concepts in the sentence to render it incomprehensible. He saw that Ardon, who often acted on reflex, had drawn his laser.

Lethor raised his hand to caution him against any unnecessary use of force. Like all Hunters, he found his sensibilities upset by purposeless violence. Meaningful violence was something else again.

The actor raised his sword as if to strike, and Ardon could wait no longer. His finger was quick on the firing stud, and a bolt of searing red light shot out. Only the haste of his shot saved the man; the stream of light passed close to one side, leaving a glowing hole in the lower edge of his cloak and charring a long, smoking groove into the planks of the stage.

"Fire," shouted one of the players as he saw the glowing light and the smoke.

"Fire!" echoed the patrons, and they began to bolt, frenzied, for the exits. Seeing the possibility of being caught in the crush, Lethor quickly held the orb out to his companion. With both their hands on the orb, their outlines began to blur, though no one in the fleeing crowd noticed.

Ellie wasn't sure how she had made it outside without getting trampled on. She felt her hip and shoulder where bruises were surely forming.

"Some jape perpetrated by a rival company," said a man standing beside her. "You know what these players are like."

That seemed as good an explanation for it as any, and since Ellie was not imaginative, that was how she would present it to Leah. She would also chaff her about missing all the fun.

Chapter
8

*T*hat evening Scorpio crept from the house unobserved. After what Leah had told him about Kelley's designs on the orb, it seemed best not to hide it in his chamber, where it might be easily found. Looking about the grounds, he saw the moon's reflection caught on the dead surface of the lake for which the house was named. Mortlake. Less a lake than a stagnant pool, its edges were ragged with reeds, and algae had turned the water dark and murky. Unseen frogs splashed a warning as he slid down the bank to the water's edge.

Dark and forbidding as it was, the water seemed to call him. He slipped from the hampering rough cloth of his monk's robes, palmed the orb and dived. He hit the water so cleanly there was scarcely a splash. His thick Aquay skin was impervious to the water's chill, and being back in his element again felt good. He spiraled to the bottom and hovered there feeling free as he never felt on dry land. As he held the orb, a warm sensation tingled his palm, and the orb's glow was cool and diffuse through the cloudy water. "Yes, we must separate again," he told it, not feeling foolish because there was so much about it that seemed alive. For all he knew, it could hear his words; if only there could be full communication. He knew the orb would be safe here, and easily recovered, at least for an Aquay. He placed the orb carefully in a slight depression in the lake bed where it half sank into the silt.

He pulled himself up the bank and donned the thick robes, feeling somewhat bereft, especially with Leah gone. She didn't understand this time any better than he did, but at least she was among her own kind. Humans were so different from him, he always felt at a loss. He did know he trusted Dr. Dee to help him if that were possible.

He nearly collided with Kelley as he returned to the house.

"Where have you been?" Kelley demanded. "The doctor sent me out to look for you. Said he had important instructions regarding the séance, though I'm not sure why. He also said he was arranging a private audience for you with the Queen, and I'm not sure why he's doing that, either. Let Gloriana get a look at that face and—you're wet!"

Scorpio felt uneasy, his mind setting up an undercurrent of warning, "Run . . . Get away . . . Flee!" as it always did in Kelley's presence. The man was as rude and arrogant as Scorpio was diffident and retiring. "I-I fell into the lake when I was walking on the grounds."

"Fell into the lake, eh," said Kelley, laughing rudely.

Since Kelley seemed so angry about something, Scorpio only followed him back to the house without saying anything else. It was better just to go along with everything for now, until he understood more of what was happening. He wondered what was meant by a "queen." Possibly a ruler of some sort, like the Pope. That made his mind flutter with warnings again, as he remembered how he'd been betrayed in Avignon. He hoped that Kelley hadn't been standing there watching all the time he was hiding the orb. Even so, he didn't think a human would dare brave those cold, murky waters. That was one of the benefits of having an eel's skin, he supposed smugly.

Dr. Dee was waiting in his study. "Scorpio, I've decided that you will aid us in our séance with de Simier tomorrow.

I think your presence will make the ritual even more impressive.''

''But I've gathered all the information you asked,'' said Kelley rather agitatedly. ''All is in readiness. Having a novice present might spoil my concentration.''

''Nonsense, Edward. You're an old hand at this by now, and I trust you to dazzle de Simier with your usual skill. Scorpio, with his unique appearance, will be just another dramatic device.''

Kelley listened grudgingly as Dee outlined his plan, daring to make no protest. He began to wonder what place this interloper might eventually earn in Dee's favor. One would think the dotard thought of Scorpio as a son, the way they put their heads together over those old books at all hours. Heretofore Kelley had enjoyed a particular place in the doctor's good graces, purely by dint of his psychic talents. It was obvious to him that with his shady background, he wouldn't have gone far as a medium without Dee's patronage. He had grown used to sharing the doctor's fame and the occasional financial gifts from the court. Occasionally, Dee got out of sorts with him because of his drinking and his temper, but he always took him back again.

Someday, he knew, he could go out on his own as a medium and be a great success, but for now, he meant to keep this situation. He'd have to come up with some clever means to discredit Scorpio. He seemed innocent enough, but who knew what was going on in that ill-shaped head. He could be plotting their deaths at this moment and no one could read it on his face.

Dim candlelight caught and flickered in the crystal as Jean de Simier and his host entered the inner chamber. Kelley was already seated at the table, dressed in a robe of fine white linen on which had been embroidered a glittering webwork of arcane symbols. Dee set about the final preparations, causing a suffumigation of bay leaves and pep-perwort to perfume the air, and carefully drawing a ''magic circle'' on the floor in yellow chalk, explaining that only within the circle would one be safe from evil spirits, should any be summoned by accident. He supposed this occult chicanery should irk him, since what he sought was the real Source, the Wellspring of all creation, but he had always been enough of a showman to enjoy this part of his work for Queen and country. The small room was close and airless, the scent of herbs attaining an almost suffocating quality, the only light a few slim candles burning in a wall sconce.

De Simier, a handsome, black-bearded fellow in a doublet of fawn brocade frothed with lace and embellished with elegant silver buttons, watched all this with a sort of patient amusement, taking out a silver snuffbox at intervals and inhaling a pinch of snuff off his wrist with a practiced, graceful gesture. He seemed to be saying he'd seen all this before and wasn't impressed.

Good, thought Dee. The Frenchman would present a stim-ulating challenge to his arts.

Dee closed the circle once they were inside it and began to intone in a sonorous voice, ''Zapkiel, Agiel, Sabathiel. Hamiel, Hagiel, Noguel. I conjure thee by the great living God, the Sovereign Creator of all things, to appear, without noise and without terror, to answer truly unto all questions that I shall ask thee. Hereunto I conjure thee by the virtue of these Holy and Sacred Names.''

As these words died into silence, Kelley began to thrash about and to moan loudly. Out of the corner of his eye, Dee watched his guest and thought he could distinguish the be-ginnings of a feeling of uneasiness. Throwing back his head, Kelley gave one last full-throated shriek for good measure and lay back laxly, his eyes glazed.

Dee raised his arms in a theatrical gesture and then

brought his hands down suddenly to douse the flames of the candles. In the scent-laden darkness, a black drape was drawn off from before a hidden alcove by a spring device. Inside the alcove stood Scorpio, his alien features brought into startling prominence. It was helpful, Dee thought, to have a working knowledge of optics, although no amount of trickery could duplicate Scorpio's face. He had been given robes similar to Kelley's, and it looked as though he'd painted his face and hands as chalky white as the linen. It made him look like a shrouded corpse with huge, staring eyes. Of course, that made it all the better. If you couldn't have real magic, Dee supposed, artificial magic by means of clever devices was the next best thing.

Kelley nearly fell off his chair from surprise, so startling was the effect. He had to hand it to the stargazer, he really knew how to put on a show.

He didn't even have to look over to see how this was affecting de Simier. He heard the man's sudden indrawn breath, his whispered *Mon Dieu* and shuffling of feet as if only fear kept him from fleeing the protection of the magic circle.

"Speak, spirit. With the lips and tongue of this poor mortal. Impart your wisdom to us."

Kelley began his usual babble, but soon lapsed into more coherent speech. They went through the questions and answers that they'd rehearsed, mostly information about de Simier's home and family, to convince him that they had knowledge by supernatural means.

He hated to admit it, but Dee had been right about the boggart. One look at that face and the froggie was ready to jump. But it worked too well. How long would it be before Dee decided he could do this show without the medium?

He knew that de Simier would blame the "spirit" and not the medium for whatever message was sent. All he had to do was to come up with the message that would cause the most trouble. Of course! De Simier's houseman had assured him that d'Alençon was still pursuing his suit for the Queen's hand from the Netherlands, and that Elizabeth had paid for his military campaign there.

"The spirit is not confined by time or space," he intoned. "I see the Duc d'Alençon in the Netherlands drinking with his officers. He brags that he has won the heart of your Queen and that it is all in jest. He cares more for her Royal Treasury than her person.

"Ohhh, I grow dizzy. The spirit leaps across the Great Water as if it were a rivulet. I see d'Alençon's mother, Catherine de Médicis, resplendent in rich garments. She is gloating over her plan to trick her enemy Elizabeth into paying for d'Alençon's campaign. How she will enjoy telling everyone of it!"

"*Mais non,* that's not true," sputtered de Simier in an incoherent mix of English and French, but the spring device had been activated again and the room was plunged into darkness.

There were muffled curses, and when finally the candles were lit, de Simier had fled, outrage causing him to break the imaginary barrier of the circle.

From his alcove Scorpio pushed back the drape and blinked out confusedly, like an owl in daylight, uncertain about what had happened and his own part in it. He looked down embarrassedly at the whiteness of his hand. Aquay skin changed color to blend in with the surroundings; thus, he'd taken on the color of the robe. It was an Aquay principle always to blend in and not to stand out. Well, it was for all but him, he supposed.

"You fool," shouted Dee. "The Frenchman's gone off in a rage, probably to tell d'Alençon about this insult."

Kelley made rude grunting noises and attempted to focus his eyes. "Wha—uh? What happened? You know how easy

I slip into a trance state when I look at the crystal. I didn't mean to, but—''

"You were entranced? Then where did that message come from?" Dee looked suspiciously at Scorpio. "I must follow de Simier and try to undo the damage somehow."

"I thought everything went well. Was there some problem?" asked Scorpio when Dee had left.

"You know these Frenchmen," said Kelley. "They get emotional over nothing. You did a fine job." Kelley was about to put a friendly arm about Scorpio's shoulders, but the Aquay's alien appearance made him think better of it.

"Now the next thing Dr. Dee wants is for you to give the Queen herself the same message as the spirit imparted to us here. I hear you'll be having an audience with her soon. Let me repeat it so you'll be sure and get it right."

Scorpio was a quick study, thought Kelley later that night. Those few insulting words to the Queen and it would be "off to the Tower." No more worries about losing his fine situation with Dr. Dee. Of course, Dee might find himself in trouble as well, but that would leave Kelley in line as Royal Astrologer, and Leah could be his assistant. He went to sleep dreaming of that pleasant arrangement.

Chapter 9

"*F*orget purse-cutting practice today," said Ellie as Leah came down from her room sleepy-eyed. "We've got some real game to stalk. Remember that fine gown you showed me? Go put it on. You've got to seem like a lady today."

Leah returned to her room and put on the yellow gown Mistress Dee had given her, feeling uneasy because she didn't know what Ellie had in mind for her to do.

"You look real fine, darlin'. You're sure to turn the young gentlemen's heads in that getup."

"I thought I was to learn to turn out their purses, not turn their heads," said Leah suspiciously, knowing how Ellie earned most of her livelihood.

"In this case it's to be a bit of both," said Ellie. They joined the foot traffic in the street, jostling their way along. Ellie's two ragged boys followed them, arguing intently all the while. "You see," said Ellie, "Sir Walter Raleigh, a fine knight and gentleman, was walking with the Queen, and when they come to a puddle of water, he whipped off his elegant cloak and put it over the puddle."

"But it would get all soiled."

"Sure it did, muddy as hell, especially since he let Elizabeth walk over it. Y'see, that allowed her to keep her feet clean."

"That seems a stupid way to treat a perfectly good cloak.

I know I wouldn't have walked over somebody's clothes.''

"But the point is that a cloak is usually a gentleman's most expensive garment; it shows how he values a lady. All of London was buzzing about it. Now everyone's competing to make grand gestures of gallantry, like Sir Walter. Whenever there's a puddle particularly, the cloaks fly.''

"I don't know why you're telling me all this. I don't have a cloak.''

"Ah, yes, that is the point, dear. You need a fine cloak to go with that lovely dress of yours, don't you think?''

They had reached St. Paul's Cathedral and had to slow their pace to thread their way through the crowd. This seemed to be a busy day here. Peddlers were taking full advantage, crying their wares in raucous voices. Customers dawdling in front of hucksters' booths, porters carrying bundles, and litters conveying ladies or gentlemen jostled for space.

"All right, look sharp now. Pick your mark, some fine gentleman of wealth, and make sure he's wearing a cloak. When you're sure he sees you, give a little girlish shiver and faint.''

"In this crowd? Someone's sure to walk over *me* like the Queen did over Sir Walter's cloak.''

"Let's get a little farther off from the crowd, then.''

Leah strolled along, pretending to stop and look at a peddler's display of ribbons, though she was feeling nervous, remembering her other attempt. She saw a tall, handsome young man with neatly trimmed brown beard and short hair in the fashion of the times, and judged his wealth by his elegant costume: doublet of burgundy velvet with long, embroidered, jewel-encrusted sleeves slit to hang behind him, a small, flat hat with an ostrich plume and a blue cloak lined in sable. Feeling awkward, since she had never done such a thing, she caught his eye and smiled, she hoped, mysteriously. He smiled back, looking somewhat amused, and made a slight bow.

Leah was suddenly flustered, feeling heat rise into her cheeks. She knew what she was planning called for coolness and calculation, but she couldn't help noticing his mischievous green eyes and wondering what he was like. You know him already, she realized. He's a gentleman of fashion, a courtier; obviously, he's as shallow and self-centered as all his kind, no matter in what century one encounters them.

As the gentleman approached, Leah had the sudden desire to turn and run, but she forced herself to stand there, a stiff smile on her face. What can I say? her mind asked desperately, and then she realized that there need be no conversation at all. They would never exchange a word; there would never be an opportunity to know him. Pretending a sudden weakness, she wilted like a flower at his feet.

She felt strong arms around her, and she let her eyelids flutter open to be sure it was the man she'd chosen. This wasn't going well, and for all she knew she'd been scooped off the filthy street by a vagabond. She let her eyes close as she recognized him. If she looked into his face, she'd surely begin to wonder about him again, and he was only a victim, a "rabbit," as Lord Foist would say.

True to Ellie's word, he was wrapping his rich cloak around her. He lifted her to her feet.

"Thank you, sir, you're a true knight and gentleman." Ellie had appeared, somehow, out of the crowd, walking and talking briskly. "Come along, child, we've got to get you home now, so you can recover. You've never been strong."

"Make haste," Ellie whispered angrily into Leah's ear as the two of them set off down the street, hoping to become lost in the crowd. The crowd obliged them, closing in around tightly until they had made their escape.

• • •

Leah ran her hand over the luxurious fur. "We did it. It was so easy!"

"I told you it'd work. Show 'em a pretty young face and you can get away with anything." Leah caught a wistful look on Ellie's weathered countenance as she said this, as if remembering better times, but then she brightened. "Let's have a bit of fun. We can slip back now and watch what happens next."

"No, we can't go back. What if he sees us? What if he calls the guard?"

But Ellie was already leading her along, and before long she saw the gentleman she had robbed, searching fruitlessly through the cathedral. "Hide here, behind this column," said Ellie, "and watch the fun."

At first, Leah was petrified that she'd been seen and probably would be arrested. Then she began almost to like the feeling of flirting with danger, and felt pride at her skill in stealing the cloak without being caught. It hadn't been as hard as she'd thought. She could almost learn to enjoy this. And she had an advantage that other thieves did not: if things got too dangerous, she could always find Scorpio and the orb, and they could jump again.

As she watched, she saw Roger and Darby creeping up on the young man from either side. As Roger burst from the crowd to shout a foul oath, dodging away as the man reached for him, Darby came up from behind and almost casually used his thin-bladed knife to separate the thongs that held the gentleman's purse on his belt. By the time he felt the tug and reached to see what had happened to his purse, Darby had fled, laughing, into the crowd.

They left the gentleman there looking foolish and angry.

"I taught the boys well," said Ellie proudly.

Leah looked at Ellie's smiling face as she beamed with pride over her sons, as much as if they'd done some noble deed she could brag about, and felt a curious detachment.

It was as if Ellie and the boys, even the gentleman, weren't real to her. As if they were players on a stage, and when the play was done, they'd go off laughing, becoming altogether different people. Then the moment passed, and she knew they were real. She was the "player," not them. Their lives were real because this was all they had, and all they would ever have.

"They were wonderful," she said a little belatedly, to answer Ellie's comment about her boys, and it seemed to please the woman.

"Let's go back and you can show Lord Foistwell your trophy; a good day's work, I'd say."

Lord Foistwell narrowed his eyes to peer at the cloak and blew on the fur to judge the luxury of the pelt. "Must admit I had my doubts about training you," he said. "Kelley hasn't ever brought me a smart one yet, but this is a good job of work, and I hope to see much more." He reached out for it greedily.

"Can't I wear it?" asked Leah. "Just for this afternoon?"

"Let her. After all, she's earned it," said Ellie. "Don't you see how handsomely it complements her gown?"

"All right, but I'll check to see if it's soiled, and if it is—"

Leah wasn't sure why she wanted to hold onto the cloak; it didn't have anything to do with the vanity of wanting to wear it, as she'd told Lord Foist. It didn't have anything to do with the triumph she'd felt earlier about separating the gentleman from his finery. It was all right to take from the rich, she reasoned; after all, they'd taken enough from her. Aimeric would have taken her virtue, without a second thought. Pope Clement had stolen her father's life and her trust, all to advance his own position. Selfishness and wealth seemed to go hand in hand, and it was only fair that she took back something. She supposed she'd complete her training as a thief, and if need be, she would steal the old Kabbalist's secret, if that was what it took to help Scorpio. But somehow she knew she couldn't keep this cloak.

It was really very strange. She supposed her early training played a part, the way her father taught the Torah and agonized over the Talmud. She had been brought up among people who trusted each other because they had no one else to trust except their own kind. When she finally boiled it down to its essence, it was simply the way having stolen the cloak made her feel. It was as if she had wallowed in filth that could not be washed away, scrub as she might. It didn't help to realize that the gentleman had only been coming to her aid. She wondered what would happen to the next person who fainted or fell ill on the street as the young man passed.

It surprised her to realize that the code that forbade theft existed not only to protect property. A human being naturally wanted to feel good about herself, and injustice hurt. The freedom she had felt earlier when she imagined skipping from one time to another whenever things got too rough dissolved like a mirage.

Returning to St. Paul's, Leah began to retrace the gentleman's path. His clothing and handsome appearance were distinctive enough so that when she described him, she discovered that he was Lord Bothwell. She remembered Dee mentioning Bothwell as a young lord who had connections at court and a rich and powerful family. If I'm going to steal, she thought wryly, it might as well be from the richest. Following the leads of several passersby, she was able to locate him at last. She walked behind him among the pillars, trying to decide what to do. She could give a street urchin a coin to return the cloak for her, thus redeeming herself without embarrassment. But considering the children she had been exposed to so far, there was no guarantee that the urchin wouldn't end up with both the coin and the cloak. That meant she would have to put it into Bothwell's hands personally, even though she wasn't sure what he'd do when he saw her again. After a few minutes she gathered up enough courage to confront him.

Lord Bothwell strode along the pavement, not looking up to see who was coming, but depending upon his bulk and his frowning expression to keep people out of his way. It had begun as a fine day, with business to finalize and a few hours of leisure to mingle with the folk at St. Paul's. Things had really become promising when the yellow-gowned wench had caught his eye. She didn't seem at all like the women who came here to show off their finery or to entice the unwary. There had been something so innocent in her expression as she smiled at him that he couldn't be sure what her intentions were. That had intrigued him; after all, he'd come here for a bit of excitement. And then after she attracted his attention, she had fainted dead away before him. Damn, he'd been totally taken in by the vixen, holding her as if she were some sort of breakable doll and hoping she'd open those huge, dark eyes and look at him again. He had felt disappointed when the harridan took her away.

It had taken him a moment to realize that he'd been relieved of his cloak as well.

Then he'd been doubly gulled when those dirty-faced brats had surrounded him kicking and cursing like sailors, and suddenly he was missing his purse. What a day!

It wasn't that he couldn't afford to lose both cloak and purse, but who wanted to be made a fool of so publicly? He'd looked around for a constable, but of course, couldn't find one. If I'd seen her and her accomplice, I would have hauled the both of them off to gaol, one in each hand, he thought miserably.

Someone was making throat-clearing noises, very near.

He reached out a hand as if to brush intruders away. But then he felt someone impertinent enough to tug at his clothing and he looked down to see . . . her. It was the girl who had run off with his cloak, and she had the effrontery to be carrying it over her arm. He had an impulse to grab her, as if he were afraid she would fade back into the crowd like an apparition. But he hesitated. She didn't seem to be going anywhere. Best hear her out.

"You left abruptly," he said in an ironic tone. "I wanted to find you, to see if you'd recovered, though I suppose the speed at which you departed should have told me something of the state of your health."

"My chaperone is a dear soul, and very solicitous of my health. She wanted to bring me home as soon as possible lest the vile humors of the streets caused me to become ill again."

"You've been ill—well, of course, I can see how sickly, how delicate you look. Roses are as pale."

"She hurried me off so quickly I hadn't time to tell her that you'd wrapped your cloak around me. She assumed it was mine." She held out the cloak to him shyly.

Lord Bothwell stood a moment, saying nothing and making no movement toward the cloak. She stole it, and now she's returning it, just like that? he asked himself. Oh, no, my girl, maybe you've got something more in mind.

"Well, perhaps it was just a foolish mix-up," he said, taking the cloak back casually, as if he had given little thought to it. "It's unfortunate that your chaperone didn't come along to properly introduce us. I'm Andrew Haver, Lord Bothwell."

"I know," she said, not bothering to confide her own name. He realized that his stare was making her quite uncomfortable. "I really can't stay," she said hastily. "My chaperone is expecting me back."

"Of course not. This is no place for a fine lady."

"You know I'm not a fine lady," said Leah, and her sudden honesty, putting a stop to the badinage, startled him.

"I'm afraid I don't know what you are," he said. This was the time to seize her, to shout for the constable. She might well be planning something even worse. It was hard for him to see her as a danger; she had the look of a startled deer. "But I might enjoy finding out, I think."

Before he finished his sentence, she had wheeled and run. For a few paces he tried to follow, but the milling mobs of the street seemed to have swallowed her up. He stopped, smoothing the fur of his cloak, remembering her dark eyes and the direct way she looked at him. London is a large city, he thought, but not so large that I can't find you again.

Chapter
10

Scorpio, Dr. Dee and Kelley waited nervously outside the audience chamber. Scorpio looked down at himself. Mistress Dee had stitched up one of her son's costumes to fit his odd physique and had padded it out until it was difficult to see his differences without looking closely. The stockings made his legs look even skinnier, but as she'd told him, "Many a man has lanky legs and is not thought the worse for it."

"Remember that the Queen loves to be flattered," said Dee. "Did you commit to memory those compliments I gave you?"

"Yes, I tried to," said Scorpio dutifully. "But what exactly is flattery?"

"Pretty lies," said Dee.

"The Queen enjoys being lied to? She must be a curious person, indeed."

"I think this is going to be a big mistake," said Kelley in an undertone, as if to himself.

"The Queen will be charmed," said Dee, sounding as if he wanted to convince himself. He was beginning to have second thoughts about Scorpio's day in court. Scorpio wasn't even human and knew nothing of the correct protocol. Who knew what he'd do to disgrace himself and his sponsor. "Here, put this on before you go in."

"What is this?" asked Scorpio, turning the mask over in

his hands and wondering what part of the body it was supposed to fit over. It was a grotesque mask, a demon face with protruding snout covered over in blue spangles that looked like scales. Two tufts of feathers at either temple resembled wildly flowing hair.

"It's to cover your scarebabe face," said Kelley. "So the Queen won't bolt when she sees you."

"This is surely uglier than I am," said Scorpio, holding the mask beside his face.

Kelley laughed. "I'd say you were twins."

"Be quiet, Edward, if you can't be encouraging," said Dee, fastening the mask behind Scorpio's head with a thong. "We mustn't upset the delicate sensibilities of the Queen. Besides, the courtiers themselves often desport themselves in masks at balls and galas. You'll be right in fashion."

After a time a servant in elegant livery opened the door and beckoned Scorpio inside.

Dee watched his protégé enter the Audience Hall with a nagging feeling of anxiety. He knew that Elizabeth could be kind, but she could also be downright capricious and cruel at times, too. She made a bad enemy. He knew he'd kept Scorpio here overlong already by promising to help him learn to control his orb device. He didn't really have knowledge of its workings, but if Scorpio made a good impression on the Queen, Dee was sure to get the funds he needed to continue his scientific studies. Who knew what he could learn if he had funds and leisure to study the orb? The Queen's meeting with his celestial visitor was a necessity, but he wished he didn't feel as if he'd just sent a lamb to the slaughter.

"The honorable Scorpio of Aquay, Keeper of the Golden Orb," the servant bellowed as Scorpio began to walk down what seemed like a mile of red carpet leading to a three-tiered dais at the far end of the room. He wondered why he hadn't simply been announced by his name. There were no titles on Terrapin, since all were Aquay. Or at least that was the case before the Hunters came.

All the way down the aisle he kept getting messages from his subconscious: *Run. Hide. Danger!* But Dee had said it was important, for some reason, to please the Queen. Scorpio gathered it had something to do with the medium of exchange on this world—something Dee called money. Dee coveted it greatly. When the Queen was pleased, she was generous with this money. Dee had told Scorpio that he needed it to continue his researches.

Scorpio was a little puzzled. This had been called a private audience with the Queen, yet a half dozen of Elizabeth's gentlemen-pensioners surrounded the dais, stoic looks on their faces and gilt axes held upright beside them. He supposed they were there to protect the Queen—from him! It made him smile, but of course they couldn't know that the Aquay were nonaggressive by nature.

Upon the second level two men stood: the ministers Lord Burghley and Walsingham, according to what Dee had told him, though he couldn't tell one from the other. They both looked like slightly weary human males of middle years, and one of them wore an implacably worried look. Upon the upper tier sat a very fancy chair. The arms and legs of it were covered in shiny, golden metal and encrusted with gems—prized as much as money here, he had observed, though an Aquay would have little use for such sparkling rocks. On the chair was a woman, also, as he judged, of middle years, legs and feet hidden by a voluminous skirt. The gown she wore was sewn with what must have been thousands of the gems here called pearls. His world had these gems, too; they were the result of a piece of grit falling into a common mollusk, not his idea of something to be treasured. And if the padded and jeweled gown of amber brocade wasn't heavy enough, several necklaces and brooches of gold and jewels helped to weigh her down even more. He got the impression of a slender, wiry, strangely dynamic woman under all the padding and had a sinking feeling that his own disguise couldn't protect him from her perceptive gaze.

Elizabeth had hair of a brighter red than he'd previously seen on a human, so he suspected it might be artificial, though artificial hair seemed a bizarre concept. (Hair seemed a bizarre idea to him, for that matter; it reminded him strongly of the tentacles of a sort of jellyfish native to Terrapin.) And her skin was preternaturally white, almost phosphorescent. He had heard Dee's wife say that the Queen soaked her skin in some sort of potion made of egg whites, alum, borax and white poppyseed. Sounded disgusting, but he found this part of her the most attractive feature, since to him most humans looked unpleasantly pink, as if they'd been boiled. As to her beauty, which was legendary here, he couldn't presume to judge, but at the moment, to him at least, she seemed quite frightening.

Trembling inside, Scorpio paused on the lowest level of the tier and knelt, in the posture he'd been shown, waiting for some sign that he could speak.

He heard a soft laugh. "So you're Dr. Dee's latest toy. You certainly seem a novel one, and I hope you're more durable than his usual offerings. He's continually trying to create mechanical toys for me, a little man that walks, a bluebird that flaps its wings, but they always break. It's so disappointing. You have leave to speak."

"I wish Your Majesty good day," said Scorpio.

A silence ensued at the rippling, high-pitched sound of Scorpio's voice. The two men looked toward Elizabeth, as if judging what her reaction would be, so they would know what to do next.

"A voice like a songbird. So lilting and musical. Say aught else so we may listen." Though there were three of them present, Scorpio had the odd feeling that the Queen somehow considered herself plural.

"Your Majesty's face is as serene and pale as the moon and assuredly as cratered," said Scorpio. That *seemed* right; he knew that Dr. Dee had written something about the moon, and he had noted that this particular satellite had definite shadows indicating crater formations. Dee had made him memorize several such speeches, each more flowery and ridiculous than the one before it, since this sort of thing didn't come to him naturally. However, under stress, he tended to forget things. In fact, he had forgotten to tell Dr. Dee about this forgetfulness.

"Our thanks, sir," she said with a certain coldness. "We were told you come from domains remote from our England. So remote as to be another world. Is this true?"

"Yes. But of all the worlds I've visited, I've seen no woman more beauteous than Gloriana, nor one with such shining . . . tentacles." No, he thought desperately, that wasn't it.

The Queen pursed her lips as if sucking a lemon. "Someday we may send our ships thither," she said.

"It hardly seems likely," said Scorpio, forgetting the next flowery speech, but he supposed it was just as well, since the flattery ploy didn't seem to be working too well.

"Don't be so sure, otherworldling. Our domain is fated to be far-flung."

Sensitive to dangerous situations, Scorpio felt the tenor of the visit change, grow more strained.

"Dr. Dee has made claims. He calls you an angel, says that you're omniscient, that you know the secrets of the universe. Can you prophesy for us?"

"I would be delighted," said Scorpio, feeling a bit trapped. What if he said the wrong thing? This world was a barbaric one, after all, and maybe there would be consequences for displeasing as well as for pleasing a queen.

Despite the foolish ceremony, he had begun to feel the gravity of this meeting. He wasn't sure that he liked this Queen, but he did realize that Elizabeth was somehow a person of substance and wit, a swift intelligence coupled with a vast power.

"I have had a surfeit of pomp and glory," said Elizabeth, relaxing a bit and falling into the singular. "As any woman, my thoughts sometimes turn to love. Shall I find a constant lover? What are my chances?"

Scorpio tried to recall more of Dee's coaching, but everything was a formless jumble. He could remember nothing. A moment of agonizing silence passed. He dared tell nothing but the truth to this commanding presence.

Mistress Dee had often told him tales of Elizabeth stopping to listen attentively to one of her subjects, even though it might be the lowliest peasant. She was sometimes rude to her servants, her courtiers, but always had time for her people. "I think that your only faithful and lasting love will be your people," he stammered, "and it's love returned. I've heard they cheer you everywhere you go and grieve over your illnesses, as if one of their children were suffering."

"My ministers have always fretted about the lack of a successor," said Elizabeth, shooting a wicked glance at Burghley and Walsingham. "Tell me, will I produce an heir?"

He remembered Dr. Dee making some remark about the Queen being past the usual childbearing age. "Your Majesty, your heirs will be a thousandfold. Heirs of your indomitable spirit, not of your flesh."

"Well spoken, strangeling. I would have been well advised if I had Scorpio of the Aquay as one of my ministers. I have yearned for the things other women have—home, husband, children—but what other woman has a kingdom and such loyal subjects? My lover will be England; my successor, my memory in the hearts of the people. So be it! The time grows short. Do you have aught else to tell me?''

In the roiling tumult of Scorpio's brain, the message Kelley had told him to deliver came floating to the surface. He didn't trust Kelley, but Dee considered him a true psychic. Maybe this message was important to the Queen. ''The spirits also speak to me of your latest suitor, le Duc d'Alençon.''

''This sounds interesting. Say on,'' urged the Queen.

''He no longer wishes to marry you. In fact, he was merely interested in your treasury so that he might finance his campaign.''

There was another strained silence in which Burghley and Walsingham looked dumbstruck at the insult.

Elizabeth burst out into laughter. ''I never had any plans to wed or bed my little froggie, so I'm glad his heart will not be broken. There is no longer any benefit to be gained from marrying the Frenchman. The price of a skirmish in the Netherlands is a small one for the pleasure of outsmarting both Henry III of France and his harridan of a mother and my dear foolish Philip II of Spain.''

''There was more, I—'' stammered Scorpio, but he couldn't remember the part about Catherine de Médicis. He hoped it wasn't important.

''You are a charming innocent,'' said Elizabeth. ''And you make me laugh. I hope to entertain you at court often. And perhaps you'll not be so coy next time and allow me to see your face. I think it may be a handsome one.''

Scorpio was about to deny this, but then realized that it was the Queen's turn to bandy flattering words. Burghley and Walsingham were nodding their agreement, though Scorpio felt it would go hard with anyone who didn't agree. Perhaps now things would work out. Dee would get his money, his researches would allow him to help Scorpio master the orb and all would end happily.

"The audience is at an end," said Elizabeth. "Tell your sponsor, Dr. Dee, and his assistant that I would be pleased to entertain all of you at dinner. You otherworldlings do eat, don't you?"

"Yes, but we don't enjoy it," said Scorpio, still in a muddle.

Elizabeth burst into peals of laughter.

Scorpio went out to join the waiting Dr. Dee and Kelley. The latter seemed distinctly peeved to see Scorpio returning, as if he hadn't expected him to come back.

"Well, did you remember all the speeches I taught you?" asked Dee.

"Your Majesty's form is as agile and lithe as a . . . mighty oak," he parroted.

"No, her *steadfastness* is as the oak," moaned Dee. "What did you say in there? What did you do? My reputation is ruined, ruined!"

"I told you not to trust the slimy eel," said Kelley. "They're probably coming for all of us right now. It's the Tower for sure. But I'm only your assistant, remember? I'm not responsible for any of this and I don't want any part in it."

"I'm not sure," said Scorpio, "but I don't believe it went so badly. The Queen invited us to dine with her; is that good?"

Dee hugged Scorpio as he wriggled to be free, his overloaded brain sending muddled messages of fear.

"It's good. It's wonderful," said Dee, dancing him around. "I knew it, you're about to become a court favorite."

"We'll have riches beyond our dreams," said Kelley.

"You're only the assistant, remember?" said Dee. "But

we'll allow you to partake of the feast, as long as you're civil to Scorpio."

As Dee went off to perfect his toilette for the coming honor, Kelley leaned threateningly close to Scorpio. "You got my message all jumbled up, too, didn't you? Or else you didn't deliver it like I told you to."

"No, I did deliver it, exactly as you said. Well, almost exactly. Her Majesty was quite amused, so I owe you my thanks for suggesting it."

Kelley's face seemed to grow quite red then, astounding Scorpio, who thought he was the only one on this world whose skin changed color.

Chapter
11

Kelley was hard at work in Dr. Dee's workshop at Mortlake. It was a large room, complete with a forge, and cluttered with tools and the bits and pieces of the mechanical toys Dee was so fond of making. Earlier that day Kelley had stormed through both Scorpio's and Leah's chambers in a fit of rage, throwing the bedding to the floor, ransacking the clothespress and trunks, all to no avail. The orb wasn't there.

Scorpio has hidden it someplace, he thought. If I had him to myself, I could get the secret from him, but now that he's a favorite of the Queen's, I can't touch him.

After pausing to calm himself, he began to wonder if the shining orb had been nothing but a cheap conjuror's trick. Just because the old man was gullible and believed the two were from outer realms didn't mean Kelley had to. If he could build something that resembled the orb, he could use it for his own séances. It would create a sensation, and he'd have no more reason to put up with Dr. Dee's crochets.

With this thought in mind, he had gone to the workshop to see if the effect of the orb might be duplicated. He had obtained some bladders from the butcher's leavings which now lay in a slimy mess on the tabletop. Into one of these, by dint of much effort, he had inserted a lighted candle, and he was trying, with great pains, to inflate the thing without extinguishing the candle. After a lengthy struggle, he managed it, and his eyes took in with satisfaction the glowing light inside the membrane, somewhat as he remembered the orb. Still, it seemed that the orb had had a certain quality he couldn't reproduce. As he leaned close to the experiment, suddenly the bladder burst and caught fire, filling his eyes with moisture and stinging smoke.

"Fire!" he shrieked, blundering about the room with his hands to his eyes. "Fire!"

After a moment, when no one seemed to be answering his summons, he stopped, uncovered his eyes and blinked. With arms folded, Mistress Dee stood in the doorway watching him. The remains of the bladder smoldered on the table, giving off a foul stench.

"What in the name of Tophet are you doing in here, Edward Kelley?" demanded Jane Dee. "The doctor will be most displeased. His whole workshop smells like flaming liverwurst."

"I was only, er, only conducting an experiment," Kelley said, trying to marshal his confidence against her intimidating stare.

"Well, I'll get you a bucket of water. I want this mess cleared away before the doctor gets home. Do you hear me, *Mister* Kelley?"

Later, as Kelley scrubbed energetically at the mess on the tabletop, he watched Mistress Dee out of the corner of his eye. I know she fancies me, he thought. And we're all alone here. What if I should pass by closely and steal a little kiss?

Scorpio sat idly in the study, thinking of the banquet with the Queen and her courtiers. It had been a festive occasion, and Elizabeth had given him the silver ring he now wore, bearing her royal seal. Dr. Dee told him that meant he had met with the Queen's favor and would receive many benefits. He was glad for Dee's sake, since it seemed to cheer him considerably, but powerful though she might be in her own realm, Elizabeth could do nothing to solve his own problem. He wished Leah were here now, so they could talk. There was no one else he could confide in. He wondered where she was. She had seemed to have some notion of how she could win the secret of the symbol from Jacob Auerman, but she hadn't told him what she had in mind.

We were so hopeful when we came here, he thought, but this world has as many dangers as the one we left. I hope she knows that, and I hope she's being careful, wherever she is, because if she doesn't come back . . .

He was surprised to find that his concern for Leah's safety was for her own sake and not just for the sake of his mission. He had told himself that everything he did on this world was only important in terms of how it would help his people, but he now realized that he was beginning to care about those he met.

He rose and wandered about the room, stopping to study a globe and then moving on to a shelf of books. On a table to one side rested a sphere of polished crystal smaller than the dark stone in Dee's séance room. He stared gloomily into it, but only saw the skewed reflection of his own face. If she doesn't come back, I must go on alone, he told himself, as long as there's still a chance I can help my people. But I feel so distant from them here. Unless I keep reminding myself of home, it's almost as if Terrapin had never existed.

I must concentrate, try to send my mind commands into this crystal. Perhaps it can tell me something of Leah. He sat in the chair beside the table and, placing a hand on either side of the crystal, fixed his eyes on it. He concentrated on Leah, hoping to form a picture of her within the glass or even to see her as she was at this moment. His eyes blurred from the strain, and he thought for a moment a cloudy picture was forming, but it quickly faded. He let his head droop to one side until it was resting on the tabletop.

He heard a rude laugh. "What're you trying to do there? I'd almost think you were trying to contact the angels if I didn't know you were one of 'em yourself. Or at least that's what the old stargazer believes."

Scorpio lifted his head, though he already knew it was Kelley. He had never seen him in a scullery maid's apron before, though, with his sleeves rolled back. There was also a fresh patch of bright red across his cheek, as if someone had struck him.

Scorpio couldn't suppress a warble of laughter. He supposed he should thank the man; it was the first time his spirits had been lifted all day.

Kelley tore the apron off himself, balled it up and tossed it away. "I forgot I still had that on," he growled. I'll teach the impudent eel to laugh at his betters, he thought, and then remembered what he'd said about not being able to touch him. Yet. "I was, um, just helping Mistress Dee with some cleaning. She likes to have me about. Claims I'm handy around the house."

Scorpio said nothing, but only peered into the crystal again in a melancholy way.

Maybe he's sick, thought Kelley hopefully, then aloud he said, "It's no use just staring into the crystal like that. You're not going to see anything. There's a trick to it. I could show you."

"I thought the crystal gazing was only what Dr. Dee called flummery. You know, the show we put on for the Frenchman."

"Well, that was done for a purpose, but that doesn't mean I don't have real psychic powers. Many times at Dee's urging I've looked into a scrying glass and gone into a trance. He always calls the spirits we contact angels, but who really knows what's out there?"

Scorpio saw the look of raw fear on the man's face when

he talked about contacting spirit beings, and realized that despite all of Dee's tricks, Kelley believed there was something to this scrying business. More than that, the man was terrified at what he might be in touch with. He simply covered the fear with bravado.

"Is it true, as you said during the séance, that the spirit of the showstone is able to move easily through all of time and space?"

"What I say during a trance state is always true. Do you think the spirits lie?"

"Is it possible to contact a world other than this one, to talk to the beings there?"

"Of course. There are no barriers in the astral realms."

"That seems rather hard to believe," said Scorpio haltingly.

"Get out of the way, there," said Kelley, taking a seat behind the crystal as Scorpio moved aside. "I'll show you, but don't become fainthearted when you hear voices from the other side."

Scorpio watched the man stare intently into the crystal until his eyes began to glaze over. Self-hypnosis, thought Scorpio. Is that all there is to it? A grown man scared to death of the things inside his own head? He thought about that a moment and decided that there were probably all kinds of things inside Kelley's head he preferred not to face. Scorpio preferred not to face them, either. He decided maybe this had gone too far and was about to reach out and shake Kelley's arm and awaken him.

"I see clumps of waving waterweed, schools of striped fish," said a voice so unlike Kelley's that it startled Scorpio. "Something like a castle made of pink coral. I see the people swimming in and out of openings in it, carrying bunches of seagrass and brightly colored flowers."

Scorpio stood uneasily by as the voice went on, describing what surely was the Festival of Harvest at Tridontia. He felt a chill; Kelley couldn't know about that. The strange voice coming from Kelley's mouth fell silent for a moment, then spoke again. "Scorpio. Scorpio. Don't forget me!" Kelley slumped over the table. Scorpio was trembling. Was he wrong, or did that sound like his friend Leandro's voice?

After a time Kelley looked up, his eyes clear. "You see, it's not a fake, after all. What did I say?"

"I-I didn't understand it," said Scorpio. "You must have been speaking in a strange celestial tongue."

"That's odd. Dr. Dee is always able to make out my messages. Now that you know my gifts are genuine, I'd be glad to teach you to do it for a very small consideration."

"I have nothing to pay you with."

"There's always the golden orb. You have it somewhere, anyway, even if you aren't telling where. Let's make a bargain. I teach you the skills of scrying, and you show me how to use the orb."

"That I can't teach," said Scorpio, "since I don't have the secret to controlling it myself. If I did, do you think I'd still be here?"

"If there is a secret to it at all," said Kelley, still half believing that the orb was only trickery. But I won't know, he thought, until I have a chance to hold it in my hands. There's something he isn't telling me about my trance, too. Even though I can't read that strange face of his, he was obviously nervous, as if I'd said something that frightened him. Still, I suppose hearing messages from the void would give anyone a fright. I'll have to get the wench back; she's the only one who can reason with him. I'll get my hands on the orb, whether it's truly magic or not, and then I'll dispatch this Scorpio just for the sheer pleasure of it.

Later, after some thought, Scorpio decided that it must have been his own desire for home that influenced the unconscious Kelley. It did have the effect of bringing thoughts of Terrapin to the surface of his mind. He wondered how he could have forgotten his home and resolved that nothing would stop him in his quest. Even if it hadn't been Leandro's voice, he would remember.

Chapter
12

*T*he Glove and Falcon was full of roisterers, and Leah was weary from answering the cries of "More ale!," "Drink here, girl." She darted about the room, saying, "Anon! Anon, sir!" She had grown skillful at avoiding groping hands while she filled the tankards without spilling a drop. Or usually without spilling any. The drinks were mostly beer and ale with colorful names—huffcap, maddog, and angel's food were some of the more polite ones. It was a rude and lewd crew that filled the tables. Ellie called the regulars maltworms; they were loafers, vagabonds, men of low reputation. Working in Lord Foistwell's establishment did make a sort of sense, Leah thought, as it gave one a good reason to move quickly, although the others had told her he used their services out of penury alone.

Slipping out when the tavernkeeper wasn't looking, she sneaked into the storeroom and hid behind a pile of full casks. She sank to the floor, exhausted. She had to have a moment to get her wits together, because she was sure Lord Foist had been waiting for her to return the cloak.

Yesterday she had been so moral, so brave, but she had been acting on impulse rather than planning things out as she should have. It was probably too much to hope that Foist's attention had been distracted by something else and that he had forgotten all about the cloak.

She was just about to return to work when Lord Foist came through the door.

"Where's my cloak, girl? You only had it on loan because of my good nature. I hope you won't come up with some weak story about losing it."

That had been the story she was going to tell. She thought fast. "I returned it."

"You what?" Foist's pale eyes narrowed, and she felt a gaze that seemed to see clear through her.

Leah backed away a step. "I returned it, but be patient a moment. It was in a good cause. It belonged to Lord Bothwell. He has great influence at court. I'm sure you've heard of him."

"Of course.. Who hasn't?"

"He was pleased to have the cloak back and was impressed when I told him I worked here for you, and you had advised me to do the honest thing."

"I know that he's influential. One could do worse than have a friend at court. Did you really tell him that about me?" asked Lord Foist.

"I swear it."

With an easy movement, Foist reached out and grabbed Leah's wrist. She felt suddenly vulnerable. Kelley was the only one who knew she'd come here, so nothing would point to Lord Foistwell if she would happen to disappear or if the body of a wayward girl bobbed to the surface of the Thames. He was quiet a moment, holding her easily, as if he knew she was sweating and he was savoring the knowledge. "That's a stupid lie," he said, "and you know it. I expected much better of you. Did you know you weren't the first girl Kelley has brought me to be trained? There have been several others, each more stupid than the one before. I don't know where he finds them.

"But you—you're not stupid. You have a delicate touch and a good mind. It's too soon to tell if you've got the thing that spoils many a promising thief, a conscience. You've got a real future here, if you don't throw it away. I know you're smart enough to be thinking that I can do whatever I want with you, and that's what I want you to think. It's true."

Among the voices from the next room crying boisterously for ale, Leah suddenly recognized Kelley's. "Yes, it's our friend Edward," said Foist, letting go her wrist. "I'll give you another chance, for his sake, but *never* cross me in anything again, or—"

Leah's hands trembled so much as she poured Kelley's ale that the drink slopped onto the table. She had the feeling that Foist's anger was only stayed by his underlying fear of Kelley. Obviously, she had just been rescued.

"Less haste, my girl," said Kelley. "I wanted a drink, not a bath. Come join me a minute, the others will spare you."

"How is Scorpio?" she asked, seating herself opposite him.

"Can't you think of a better greeting for me than that?" asked Kelley. "After all, I'm the one who set you up here."

Leah pushed a strand of hair off her wet forehead. "Yes, thanks for this," she said with a wry smile.

"Don't blame me, you're the one who wanted to enter Lord Foistwell's school."

"I'm sorry. It was kind of you to introduce me. I'm doing well; my training goes well. Want to see the 'clip and run'?"

"No, no thanks. You don't have to sweat here in this dirty tavern, you know. You could go anywhere you desired, if you only had the orb."

Leah remembered that she had told Scorpio to hide the orb. This made it rather obvious that he had done so, and successfully. "I don't know where it is," she confessed. "And, besides, it belongs to Scorpio."

Kelley covered Leah's hand on the tabletop with his and

leaned close to speak to her. Leah had to force herself not to pull away, remembering that in this place Kelley was actually her protector.

"But he trusts you. He would tell you where it is in a minute, if you only asked him. You're too pretty to be traveling companion to the likes of him. Get me the orb and I'll take care of him for good. With the golden crystal and my powers as a medium, our fortune would be made. Think of it—living like royalty with all of London at our feet."

Leah lowered her gaze, feigning shyness. That way she didn't have to say either yes or no.

Kelley smiled fatuously, as if he had her exactly where he wanted her. "Of course, a dainty thing like you can't make a quick decision. I can be patient. But in the meantime, Dee took our goggle-eyed friend to see the Queen, and for some reason she liked him and invited him to dine. I think he may have cast a spell upon her."

"He's been to see the Queen?" asked Leah. "But I wanted to—" Kelley looked at her. Of course. She wanted to see if Elizabeth was as beautiful as everyone said, and if she wore a gown dripping with gemstones.

I wanted to ask her, Leah thought, what it's like to be a ruler and a woman, and how she can bring herself to sign someone's death warrant. I would have told her how much it frightened me to think I might be responsible for a patient's life.

"You would have loved the banquet," said Kelley. "The yeomen of the guard, bareheaded and with scarlet livery with a golden rose on their backs, came in bringing a course of twenty-four dishes served in gold plate. There was a dish with a peacock roasted and then cunningly presented in his feathers so that he appeared alive again. Such a surfeit of dainties, I don't know what all. Each yeoman was given a morsel from the dish he had brought, since Her Majesty is always in danger of being poisoned.''

"It all sounds charming," said Leah, imagining what it would be like not to freely eat one's food. Yet rulers, women or not, had to live with the realities of power.

"I wish you could have gone with me; you would have been a great success."

She looked down at the shapeless gray gown the tavern wenches were given to wear, the splotches of ale drying on it. Scorpio was at court yesterday dining with the Queen, she thought, while I was scrubbing this alehouse floor.

"Like I said, missy," murmured Kelley persuasively, "you can be rid of Scorpio anytime you say." He cracked the knuckles of his big hands, as if he were breaking someone's bones—and enjoying it.

Kelley's crude gesture brought Leah's thoughts back to the present. If Scorpio went to see the Queen, it was with good reason, not just to be entertained. He's doing his part as I must do mine, she thought. But if I can, I must return to Mortlake and warn Scorpio of how dangerous Kelley really is.

"I think you know I'm a patient man," said Kelley, cupping Leah's chin roughly in his hand and making her look at him. "But I can't wait forever for your answer. Think it over. I'll be back soon for your decision."

He rose hastily and left. Leah scrubbed at her face with the cloth she used to wipe off the tables, trying to get rid of the feel of Kelley's fingers. Cries from the "maltworms" finally made her jump up to do her duty. She poured ale distractedly, wondering what she would do when he came back.

The following day Leah was stalking an obese gentleman under the stern eyes of Roger and Darby. She had been following him down the street, and now she moved faster

to gain on him. She watched a temptingly full pouch bob
at his hip and palmed her thin-bladed knife. I'm really going
to do this, she told herself in amazement, and then a coach
rumbled by so close it nearly hit her. She threw herself out
of the way just in time, but sat down abruptly in a puddle
of mud and offal at the street's edge. Where was that Sir
Walter Raleigh when a girl really needed him, she thought
wryly, and saw that the coach was a fine one, drawn by six
matched black horses, the royal seal outlined in gold on the
coach's side. The Queen, she thought. If I'm not to meet
her, at least maybe I can see what she looks like.

Roger yelled something as she got to her feet and sprinted
off down the street, holding her dripping skirt away from
her legs. She darted into an alleyway so she could cut the
coach off at the next corner and possibly get a peek in the
windows.

She was both disappointed and excited when she saw that
the occupants of the coach were Dr. Dee, Scorpio and Kelley. They were evidently on their way to Whitehall. I've
got to warn Scorpio she thought, but how? I can hardly go
to Whitehall like this. She looked at her torn and soiled
gown.

As the coach was about to disappear from view, she saw
it slow down. The door opened and a burly figure leapt to
the street. Kelley. He must be on his way back to the tavern
for her answer.

Only she wouldn't be there to give it.

I've wasted enough time, she thought. And I'll never be
a better thief than I am now. Too bad there's not time to
say goodbye to Ellie and the boys.

Determinedly, she set out for the Jewish quarter.

Chapter
13

*S*corpio and Dr. Dee were in Dee's study, hemmed in by stacks of books and papers. Scorpio thought that Dee was in a sort of ecstasy amid the smell of moldering old paper and the sight of crabbed writing in faded brown ink. There was a certain comfort in the room, especially since he knew the wind blew keenly outside. A friendly fire crackled on the hearth, and the only sound for some time was the brittle turning of a page or Dr. Dee's muttering as he puzzled over a Kabbalistic symbol.

Scorpio had trouble concentrating on them. He could have sworn he'd seen Leah yesterday from the coach; it had looked so like her, but this woman had been wearing a ragged and filthy gown, and there were smears of soot on each cheek. Would Leah be wandering the streets disguised as an urchin, he wondered, and if so, then why? She had asked that he trust her, but she hadn't bothered to explain whatever plan she had in mind. He had gathered that London had more than its share of thieves, tricksters and the like. Thinking of Leah among them gave him an uneasy feeling.

"Don't you understand what he's saying here?" asked Dr. Dee, shoving a book toward Scorpio.

"No," said Scorpio.

"Oh, that's right, it's Leah who reads Hebrew."

"Is that important to understanding how to use the orb?"

"Well, I don't know as yet. It's a very important bit of

information, which I'll copy into my notebook for further study.'' Dr. Dee set to his copying work with zest as Scorpio watched. Dee was in love with knowledge for its own sake, and he would gladly wade through all the ancient texts whether or not any reference to the orb ever appeared. Though Dee had a mind that questioned, as opposed to the Pope's closed one, Scorpio felt that the doctor was still far distant from any real understanding of the orb. It had felt good, for a while, to work side by side with Dr. Dee, and no doubt Dee meant well, but there was no point in deluding himself. If he wasn't careful, he could end his days as a sorcerer's apprentice, and that would do his people no good.

Scorpio knew that his presence at court also added luster to Dr. Dee's reputation as a mage. It could become addictive to be the latest wonder in the glamorous court of the Virgin Queen, but Elizabeth was notoriously fickle, and the wonder would surely fade.

If anything had been learned in his studies with Dee, it was that the mind was a powerful tool. He knew that the orb had properties that made it seem a living thing, and since it could not speak or hear, the only way to enter into a communion with it was through concentration.

He found himself often walking by the lakeside, looking down into the moving water's surface dappled with sun and shadow and directing his thoughts toward the orb, where it lay on the bottom of the lake. One day he crouched on the bank for almost two hours, sending out questing tendrils of thought. It seemed an idle exercise, since nothing had ever come of it, but this time he was determined, and he kept at it until his brain was fogged with fatigue.

It was as if his thoughts were a searching hand, groping through the murk and mud of the bottom. A chill began at the base of his spine as he felt the imaginary fingers of his mind close on something—something round and solid, not cold as it should have been from its immersion in the frigid waters, but with an organic warmth, as if he held something frail and living within his hand.

Exhaustion numbed his mind, and he couldn't hold the thought; it was as if the fingers stiffened, threatened to drop the precious burden. He concentrated until thought became actively painful. He knew he couldn't hold the connection much longer, if it really was a connection.

How do I know? he asked himself in anguish, and as he asked, he saw a gleam of light ride the ripples in toward the shore. At first he thought he had imagined it, but no, it was there—cool, steady light radiating from deep within the lake, distorted and moved by the sluggish surge of water toward the bank. He let the thought go then and collapsed on the soft mud of the shore, knowing that for the first time he had actually communicated with it, if only for a fleeting second.

I must tell Leah, he thought. But how can I? I don't even know where she is. If there was only some way to contact her. He tried to send his thoughts spiraling out to wherever she was, but he was exhausted and couldn't hold the concentration. His head throbbed from the effort.

He picked himself up from the bank, brushing away mud and twigs. The Dees were going to begin wondering about all the time he spent out by this lake. I'll get some rest, he decided, and try again later.

Kelley had been watching Scorpio as he sat by the lakeside. He had often seen him come here and stare into the water as if he considered it some sort of huge crystal. He knew that some mediums did scry by means of a vessel of water, though he'd never heard of using an entire lake. The day was chill and Kelley wrapped his cloak about himself as he thought of the coldness of the murky depths. So the fool likes to stand by this dead lake and stare, he thought. That doesn't mean I must waste my time watching him. I could be by the fireside now, with a cup of mulled cider. Still, he kept his place, just out of sight behind a leafless hedge.

He remembered the first time he'd found Scorpio near the lake. He had surprised him coming back to the house dripping wet, having fallen into the water. It would have saved me a great deal of trouble if he had drowned that day, Kelley mused. At first it was only an idle thought, and then he began to wonder if Scorpio could swim. He suddenly realized he didn't have to give him that chance. If he fell in once, he could do so again. Kelley laughed under his breath as the thought occurred to him. No, he dared not. It was too bold, and of course, he didn't have the orb. Still, the girl might know where it was by now. She'd disappeared so mysteriously. Once Scorpio was out of the way, he could have the secret from her easily enough, and he didn't think he'd have such a good opportunity again.

His brain was sluggish, but his body was already moving him toward execution of his hastily made plan. He had begun to worm his way down the hillside, keeping to cover when possible, though his quarry wasn't really looking in his direction, anyway. He had come very close when he stepped on a stick that snapped, and Scorpio looked up and saw him.

Kelley thought he read surprise in those bulging eyes. All of the indignities he'd suffered over the past weeks suddenly boiled to the surface of his mind, and he blamed Scorpio for all of them. As always, when his temper flared, he did things he wouldn't be sure about later, but he did remember leaping forward to grab the creature by his skinny arms. Kelley discovered that there was surprising strength in that whiplike body. For a moment he thought he might have made a mistake, as Scorpio almost broke free of his grasp, but he hung on and proved the stronger. He felt all resistance give way as he began to push Scorpio toward the bank. They both went in with a splash, but by his superior strength, Kelley was able to hold his enemy under the water, even though Scorpio's arms and legs thrashed about fiercely. Kelley held him down for a long time, until he began to feel the chill of the water through the blood heat of his fading temper.

As always after one of these bouts, he came back to himself and looked around at the damage that had been done as if someone else had done it. Even drowned, the Aquay's body was too warm to his liking. He pushed the limp thing in his arms as far away as he could into the water's depths. It floated there a moment, looking rubbery and lifeless, and slowly sank. Only now beginning to feel fear, Kelley sloshed to the bank and fled. Like many things that had been done in the heat of his anger, Kelley half regretted the murder. Not that he wasn't happy to be rid of the imposter, but Dr. Dee was very clever about these things. If he found out, their long association and Kelley's psychic talents might not be enough to keep Dee from telling the authorities. Reflexively, Kelley reached for the side of his head. Murder was murder, he supposed, even of a semihuman entity. He sat up late, worrying, and in his dreams, black waters closed over his face, and he thrashed against their icy coils for what seemed like most of the night.

Chapter
14

Not bothering to return to
Lord Foistwell's for fear of meeting Kelley, Leah continued
on to the Jewish quarter. Her dress was muddy and torn,
but that would go along with her plan. Rather than approaching Auerman's house from the front, she made her
way around the newly built structures beside it and came
up to the back door.

When she knocked, the same tiny, wrinkled woman appeared. She had a face like a little withered apple and, Leah
suspected, a no-nonsense attitude. Leah had wrapped a kerchief around her hair and kept her head bowed, in hopes
she wouldn't be remembered from the earlier visit. She also
kept her voice to a timid whisper.

"What is it, girl? My old ears can't understand what
you're muttering there," said the woman.

"I said I'm hungry and I'd be willing to work to earn a
few pence to buy myself a meal."

"Begging, is it? I've never seen you around here before.
Where do you come from?"

"I'm Leah de Bernay," she said, glad to be able to fall
back into her own identity. "I've newly come from Avignon, escaping the persecution there. I'm very strong and
I'd work hard."

"You don't look so very strong to me," said the woman
as she grudgingly opened the door. "But I suppose I can

find a little work for one of our own. I'm Esther Green."

Leah followed her inside and found a kitchen little changed from the one in which she'd worked side by side with Grandmère Zarah. Burnished copper kettles, along with other equipment—pot hooks, frying pans, spits, graters, gridirons and the like—hung along one wall within easy reach. In a large stone fireplace something bubbled in a pot hung just above the flames. Antique cupboards occupied another wall, and bunches of leeks and dried herbs were suspended from the high ceiling beams. Leah had been turning into a pretty fair cook, according to Grandmère, until her studies with her father began to take up so much of her time. She was sure it would all come back to her.

"I suppose you could handle the dusting and polishing," said Esther Green, handing her a cloth and leading the way to the next room. Leah worked quickly and efficiently, rubbing the carven wood to a glow. She paused before Jacob Auerman's ornate study door. "Oh, my, no," said Esther. "The master would have a fit if anything were disturbed in there. And you don't want to go in, anyway, girl. My master's a magician, and you wouldn't want to know what goes on in his study."

Leah tried to look properly awed. "Black magic?" she asked.

"Good heavens, no! The master is a devout man, very learned. But see you stay out of his way; he would have no patience with a chit of a girl like you."

Leah nodded obediently, and Esther seemed pleased. She took Leah back into the kitchen and ladled out a bowl of stew from the pot over the fire. "Here, you said you were hungry."

Leah was hungry by now and found the stew delicious. "I suppose you have no place to stay," said Esther.

"No, I—"

"You can stay here for a few days and do some work I

have planned," said Esther. "This is a lonely sort of house, with just myself and the master. I hope you won't mind."

"No, no, I won't mind. And thank you."

Esther insisted on replacing Leah's coarse tavern wench's gown with one of her own stiff black dresses. For several days Leah worked about the house, keeping her eyes averted shyly when Jacob Auerman happened to come into the room, hoping that he wouldn't remember her from her previous visit.

But the oddest thing was that after a while Leah didn't feel she was playing a role, really. Her whole upbringing, except for the fluke of her father teaching her medicine, had prepared her to fit into a proper household. She had to admit she was more at ease here than in the Dees' fine mansion. It felt comforting to lapse back into this familiar way of life.

Each week the Sabbath began with light and wine. Auerman put aside his studies and consultations, Esther her assiduous housekeeping, and the three of them gathered for prayer and worship. As a child, Leah had always been certain that on the Sabbath she would get attention from her mother and father that she sometimes didn't get during the week. At the time, that was all it meant to her, yet there was a strong lesson in seeing everything of the workaday world unfailingly put aside for a day of rest and thanksgiving for blessings received. During the rest of the week, the family might be pulled in several different directions, there might be arguments, tempers lost, but the Sabbath drew them together again and made them know how lucky they were to have each other.

She supposed that remembering these things, now that her family was dead, should have been intensely painful, but she began to find a sense of peace in the slow pace and silence of the Sabbath. Six days for energy and achievement, the seventh for contemplation; it seemed a healthy idea.

As she enjoyed her time in Auerman's house, somewhere in the back of her mind was the knowledge that she had come to despoil the place, to rob Jacob Auerman of his precious secret. She pushed it further back as the days passed. She didn't have to do anything about it until Auerman gave her an opportunity, and so far he had not done so.

Lord Bothwell strolled through St. Paul's, feeling uneasy after what had happened to him there previously. He had sent some men out in search of the raven-haired young woman, but they'd returned saying they'd learned nothing of a girl who might have been a thief or in league with thieves. He wasn't a puling schoolboy, but he still thought of her occasionally and indulged his fantasies.

It was a fine day, and he met several congenial people he knew, so the events of last time had been pushed to the back of his mind, when he saw a prim figure approaching. Dark, severe dress, head covered, basket on arm, the very picture of the proper Jewish housewife . . . except he knew her. It was the girl who had stolen his cloak. Wasn't it? For a moment he hesitated to approach her, and then she seemed to see him, and there was no need to, because she was walking straight toward him.

"Good day, madam," he said stiffly.

Leah couldn't understand his discomfiture at first, then she realized that her whole image had changed from the time she last met him. She wondered what he thought of her now. "You wanted to know who or what I was," she said. "Well, I'm Leah de Bernay. Now you know who and what!"

Her words sounded like a challenge, but she wouldn't take them back.

"I did want to know," he said. "After you ran off with

my cloak and your friends took my purse, it was hard to forget you. Can I be sure you're who you appear to be now?''

Leah smiled in spite of herself. ''Perhaps not, your lord-ship.''

''Andrew,'' he said.

As they strolled along, they passed the wooden podium that was often used to make announcements. A man stood behind it now. He was wisp-thin and his skin was so pale as to be almost translucent, colorless hair flying wildly around his face as he gesticulated. With his body so ema-ciated, it seemed as if he were powered only by the mad light in his eyes. In a quavering voice he was exhorting the passersby, and several had stopped to listen, with more joining them all the time.

''Witches can be anybody. Your next-door neighbor, the tavernkeeper, a porter in the street. But in private when no one sees, they call on Satan himself.'' Leah saw that his words were beginning to inflame the listeners, who looked about one another with frantic eyes, as if trying to see a witch mark on the man or woman beside them.

''Satan is an abomination, worse than the Black Death, and the witch is a Plague-carrier that must be wiped out, ere our souls become sick unto death!'' The speaker con-tinued in this way until he had the crowd shouting encour-agement and milling about angrily.

''I don't like the look of this,'' said Bothwell. ''There have been several riots in the last month where mobs ran about, destroying the property of those they considered witches, and this fellow seems to be inciting to violence at this moment. I think I'd better get you out of here.''

Keeping himself between her and the growing mob, Both-well hurried her along until they'd outdistanced the danger. When it was clear they were safe again, she remembered that Bothwell had connections at court. Maybe this would

be the way to contact Scorpio. "I wonder if you'd do me
a great favor. You're familiar with Queen Elizabeth's astrologer, Dr. John Dee?"

"Astrologer and sometime spy," he said, studying Leah
with narrowed eyes. "Do you know him?"

"Yes, and it's important that I send him a message. Could
you take it to him?"

"This begins to sound like some sort of plot," he said
teasingly.

"It's harmless, really. I have a friend staying with Dr.
Dee, Scorpio by name. I would like for him to meet me
here, at St. Paul's in three days' time."

"Yes, the mysterious Scorpio, man from another world.
The court is buzzing with it."

"You believe he's from another world?"

"I believe the Queen is entertained by the idea, and
anything that makes the Queen happy is the truth for the
hour. But what connection do you have with him, I wonder?"

"We are friends. You must have friends."

"One or two, when I'm not at my disagreeable worst."

"Then you'll tell him?"

"For a favor in return."

"What sort of favor?"

"Just the pleasure of your company."

"I thought that's what you were getting now."

He laughed. "I have a carriage. What'll it be? The Bear
Garden? A play?"

Leah remembered her first tour of London. "Why not a
voyage down the Thames?"

"A perfect choice."

When she saw the gaily decorated wherries bobbing at
the quayside, Leah felt excitement. She chose one with a
red-striped awning and fringes of silver. As the oarsman

pulled the boat out onto the rapidly flowing water and the bank receded behind them, she began to worry that this might not be such a good idea. Bothwell pulled her playfully back onto the cushioned seats with him, and she wondered why she chose to be here with him now, when she had been terrified of being alone and far from shore with Kelley. She knew Kelley a great deal better than she knew this man. All she knew of Bothwell for sure was that he had made the gesture of wrapping his cloak around a stranger who had fainted in the street. Would Aimeric have done any less? Just another scapegrace with more gallantry than substance, she thought, remembering Aimeric. But I discovered that flattering words and grand gestures don't always make a man.

"You seem as if you're a thousand miles away," said Bothwell.

"And a few hundred years while we're at it," she said, smiling and undoing the kerchief about her hair. The breeze was good, and the smell from the water wasn't so bad when the wind was blowing stiffly. She saw a flotilla of swans making its graceful way along the distant bank.

Andrew drew closer, and at the moment he leaned over to kiss her, she realized she knew something like this would happen. Their lips met softly for some moments, and then he drew back. She had wanted this to happen, she realized. Living out of place and time, running the streets of London with thieves, had brought out her reckless streak. But still, she'd been taught that physical love was barren without its proper setting—commitment, home, children—and as Bothwell became more ardent, she drew away. Amazingly, the title of "gentleman" he bore was more than just a word. He released her gently.

"There's plenty of time for us," he said.

Leah was silent as they drifted past the notorious Tower of London, a forbidding monolith of weathered gray stone.

From the water, everything was quiet, no rumble of traffic, no cries of street vendors. London was a dream city, slowly passing down the time-stream. She knew somehow that what he had just said was wrong. She didn't belong here and didn't think she'd be here forever. So they really had very little time to get to know each other. A tear slipped from beneath her eyelid and made its way down her cheek. She wiped it away quickly so that Bothwell wouldn't see.

The rest of the ride was spent in conversation, and Leah was in better spirits by the time they arrived back at the quay. Bothwell brought her hand to his lips and wished her farewell, but only, as he said, "until our next meeting."

Leah considered that idea, her cheeks burning, all the way back to Jacob Auerman's, but then she turned her thoughts to more practical matters. I've spent a whole afternoon daydreaming and lollygagging, she thought, and Scorpio's still in danger. Maybe Andrew will deliver my message at court, and maybe he won't. I wish there were some way to contact Scorpio. We should have arranged something before I left. Dr. Dee set great store by telepathic messages. I wonder—

I don't know where my common sense has gone, considering such a course, she thought, but it can't really hurt anything to try.

The next day Leah was scrubbing the walls in Auerman's parlor and thinking how foolish she must have looked sitting in her cubbyhole of a room and concentrating on getting a message through to Scorpio. She hadn't gotten anything but a headache from it. As she approached the door to Auerman's study, she heard a regular, rasping sound. She looked around to see if Esther was nearby, then placed her ear to the heavy door. The sounds continued. They sounded like the deep, resonant breaths of one peacefully asleep and snoring.

She pushed on the door and found it open. This was risky. If she was wrong—

But she saw Auerman lying forward on his desk fast asleep, his nose pressed against some text he'd been deciphering. This was the only chance she'd been given to get her hands on the amulet. At his throat she could see the thin cord from which it descended.

Esther had given her a small scissors to use in her needlework, and that now hung from her belt in an enameled case. With the training she'd had, it should be a simple matter to clip the cord and make away with the amulet.

It would have been simple when she first came here, worming her way into Esther's good graces. But when she was accepted, she'd fallen back into the old traditions. Perhaps these came too easily to her. She had hardly believed she would miss a way of life that promised to keep her tied to a kitchen for the rest of her days, but she had to admit that there were things about life here that were quite satisfying.

She had now been here long enough to know how much Auerman prized the secret symbol in his amulet. Every evening she brought him prayer shawl and phylacteries, and he would take out the slip of parchment, fragile and yellowed. She would see his wrinkled old face intent in the glow of flickering candles—the *merkabah* rider, ascending to spiritual heights by means of meditation.

Leah knew she had to act quickly. There wouldn't be that many chances, and everything was going according to plan, yet still she hesitated.

To take his amulet from him would be like stealing away a bit of his soul, and she couldn't do it.

First the cloak and now this. I'm a total failure as a thief, she thought.

It was a moment before she realized that Auerman's eyes were open. He straightened in his chair and stretched. Although he acted startled to see her, she had the distinct impression that he'd been watching her for a while.

"I'm sorry I disturbed you," she said, backing toward the door.

"You did not disturb me," he said. "I was deep in study, that's all."

"I'll return to my work."

"There's time for that later. Stay awhile."

"Your study frightens me," said Leah, playing the part.

"No, I don't think it does," he said. "I think it fascinates you, or at least you seemed interested that first day when you came here accompanied by those charlatans."

"I didn't think you remembered."

"Well, I'll admit, I wasn't sure you could be the same girl I remembered. When I first met you, you seemed quite unnatural. You knew how to read, and worse, you used your knowledge to contradict your elder. Then I saw you in a whole new light: doing your proper work and making the house more cheerful with your presence. I wondered at first what brought you here, but I see now that you were only out of place and needed to fit yourself back into the natural order of things. Esther has been very pleased with your work, and you've made her less lonely for a time. But I think you won't be with us much longer."

"I've been happy here," said Leah, this time not playing a part. "Your natural order of things won't ever be quite right for me again, but it's good to remember that for every path one takes, another, equally worthy path goes untraveled. That doesn't keep one from choosing a way, but it does tend to teach humility." As she spoke, she seemed to see the eyes of the women in the baths at Avignon, and she would no longer be haunted by them. They'd conveyed their message.

"I hope you'll stay long enough to help me with some of my translations."

"You'd let me?"

"I don't see why not. Since by some mischance you've been taught to read, it would be wasteful not to use the talent. I know that you read Hebrew. Tell me, what of your Latin?"

"I'm fair at Latin and Greek and even better at Provençal."

"You speak Provençal? You're not just a prodigy, but a wonder!" Jacob seemed very excited about this discovery, but she thought that she had been about as bold as she dared for the moment. "Perhaps I'd better see if Esther needs help preparing dinner," she said.

"Yes, yes, perhaps you should," he said, but he still wore a satisfied smile.

Leah was happy now that she didn't have to hide her desire to learn. She and Auerman labored over translations the next morning, and in the afternoon she helped Esther with the housework. But she began to have a restless feeling as she worked, and she didn't know why. Thoughts of Scorpio began to resonate in her mind until she couldn't think of anything else. Scorpio in danger from Kelley, deep in conversation with Dr. Dee, or just looking wistfully down at the glowing orb. Finally, she began to realize that maybe the idea of telepathy wasn't just foolery, after all. Maybe two minds that tried to seek each other out could relay a message. She resolved to find a quiet time that evening so she could be "open" to such a message if it came.

In one of the poorer districts of London, Ben Bright was going fishing. It was near midnight, he judged, as he ambled down the narrow lanes between cottages ranked in silence and shadow, carrying across his shoulder a long pole with a small hook at its tip. A fog had crept in, as it was wont to do of nights, and lay in the low places like cotton wool, but that didn't bother Ben. By the lord mayor's edict, lanterns were to be hung on the houses to lighten the gloomy streets, but especially in the poorer quarters this was not done. The streets were left to whoever dared walk them—usually folk like Ben Bright.

He crept up to the window of a cottage and waited there a moment to be sure there was no sound within. Surely, all the folk were abed by now. The window had been carelessly left open, and Ben thrust the long pole within. He had spent the last few days walking along these lanes, peering into this or that window to see what valuables might be lying about, especially those made of cloth. He also noted which householders were careless enough to leave their windows open occasionally.

Aha, thought Ben, as he withdrew the pole, landing a linen tablecloth. A fence will give me a good price for this.

Times being poor in the countryside, Ben had come to London to seek his fortune. He was one of a number of sturdy beggars and rogues who earned their living any way they could, as long as it didn't entail work of any sort.

He knew men who would put rat's bane on their flesh to create sores. Wrapping their limbs in bloody rags, they would go about begging. Himself, he was an Abraham man, someone who pretended to be mad. The clothes he wore were filthy and so tattered they left his arms and legs bare. His hair was as matted as a bird's nest. Country housewives often gave him food as a bribe to get him out of their sight, but he got his best effect by sucking on a piece of soap so that he could throw a frothing fit in front of some poor wretch of good conscience and full purse.

His attention full upon maneuvering his pole to see whether he might hook a plump velvet cushion he had seen earlier, he felt himself gripped firmly by two large hands. Such hands he supposed a constable might have, though how anyone could have slipped up on him he didn't know, since he prided himself on his keen senses.

He was just about to attempt some excuse for his actions when he felt himself, of a sudden, lifted clear of the ground as no constable would be capable of, Ben being a substantial sort. Speechless, he found himself carried like a babe in arms down the sleeping streets. He thought he heard his captor cursing or muttering under his breath in some foreign tongue as he strode along.

Ben was carried in through the courtyard of an old inn, long since fallen into disrepair and abandonment, and was deposited on the littered floor. He landed with a thud. Ben looked around furtively. There was a light in the room, though its glow was of low intensity and far steadier than any lamp should have been. There were two figures, indistinct in the dim light. The larger, the one who had brought him here, was moaning as if in pain. Quickly, he went to the strange lamp and began to rub it over his skin, sighing in relief as he did so.

"Damnable climate," said the smaller one. "The dampness of these fogs set our skin afire."

Now that he had had a moment to collect his thoughts, Ben sat up. "This ain't no pageant," he said raspingly, in a voice that had terrified many a country housewife. "So why have the two of you tricked yourselves out like the Lord of Misrule or some other devilish creature?" They were dressed identically, like mummers at a celebration, in black robes and masks of red lacquer.

"At least he speaks," said the smaller figure. "Some you brought me could only babble, and the rest knew nothing at all. I hope we do better this time, but you certainly chose a poor specimen."

"No one else was abroad."

"No matter, as long as we can question him." The figure came nearer, light playing off the shiny surface of his face—

of his mask, Ben assured himself. He knew that what he was seeing had to be some kind of disguise, but it made the hair stand up on the back of his neck all the same.

"We have come in search of Scorpio the Aquay. He may be accompanied by a female of your species. Do you know if he is in London?"

"I know nothing of this Scorpio," said Ben, hedging to gain time. It seemed he had heard that name recently in idle tavern gossip.

The mummer reached down and grabbed Ben by his ragged garment and began to shake him until Ben felt like a rat in the jaws of a terrier.

"Scorpio . . . He's the famous . . . celestial . . . traveler . . . at court . . . The man . . . from another world," said Ben between bounces, repeating the rumors he had heard about the Queen's latest prodigy.

"So where might we find this otherworldling?" The shaking stopped, but it only brought that nightmare face into greater focus, making Ben turn away rather than look at it.

"Everyone knows that he's with Dr. Dee." A hand grasped his ragged clothes again. "At his home at Mortlake in Surrey," Ben added hastily.

"At last we can finish our quest and get out of this hellish climate."

As the figure turned, the robe flared and Ben got a look at the thing's feet. It was no wonder he had heard no footfalls. The foot, split into two nailless toes in front, was soled in a spongy layer of what looked like thick callus.

No longer able to assure himself that the beings were only men in strange disguise, Ben shrieked and rolled into a ball. He was still lying there, mumbling to himself, when the two left a few moments later, though he heard no door open or close. The worst thing was, he told himself, that when Ben Bright the madman tried to tell the authorities what he had seen, no one would believe him.

Chapter
15

*T*he next morning Kelley came whistling to the breakfast table. He knew there were clouds in the sky, with rain threatening, but to him it was a beautiful day. No more eel threatening my position with Dr. Dee, he thought. Everything is going to be—As he sat down, he looked across the table and saw . . . Scorpio. Kelley sat there staring dumbly until Mistress Dee reminded him it was impolite to stare. And not only did Scorpio not look dead, he looked positively cheerful, as he set upon an immense breakfast. "What's the matter with you, Edward?" asked Dee.

"Yes, is there a problem?" asked Scorpio, fixing Kelley with his protuberant green eyes. Except for the murderous intent of the man, Scorpio had felt the whole thing was somewhat of a joke. It was hard to kill Aquays by drowning, since they could stay underwater for much longer than a human being. As soon as he had realized what Kelley intended, he played along, pretending to be the weaker, though there was a great deal of wiry strength in his slim body. He had thrashed about and then went limp, and by the look of the man's face, he had been completely fooled.

This isn't happening, Kelley told himself. He's dead. He has to be dead. I drowned him. I remember it. He looked at his hands and remembered the struggles.

"Care for some conger in sauce?" asked Scorpio, passing a dish.

How could someone clearly dead now be alive? Kelley studied Scorpio with narrowed eyes. Could he be a master conjuror and not just a fake? But what sort of powers must a man have to return from the dead? Kelley racked his brain trying to remember the incident, but since it had happened in a fit of anger, he had problems bringing it back in clear detail. Is it possible, he wondered, that being angry at Scorpio, I dreamed it all? Sometimes when the anger takes me, I have almost no memory of what occurred. It may have been only a particularly vivid dream. In fact, since Scorpio still does everything that the living do, that must be what happened. But it was so real!

Later that day Scorpio sat beside the lake, letting his mind fall into a state of utter relaxation. He replayed the breakfast scene in his mind, much to his own amusement, though he supposed that someone hating him enough to try and commit murder wasn't really a laughing matter. Still, there had been someone trying to kill him for some time now, and he was almost getting used to the feeling.

Leah had been in his thoughts a lot this morning, too. He saw her preening in the yellow gown Mistress Dee had given her; running through the streets in ragged garb; mourning the death of her family. This was the first time today that he'd had the opportunity to be alone and really try to send out his thoughts. He had learned a little more about the technique of it after that first time when he'd exhausted himself. It was better to let the mind float, as one floats on water. He watched a dead leaf rock on the lake's surface and let the thoughts of Leah flow through his mind unimpeded. He wasn't sure whether they were his own thoughts or not.

After a time, behind the images of Leah, he thought he

saw a familiar background appearing. It was fragmentary at first. Stately pillars, impressive windows, an architecture of arches and soaring towers, like a cathedral. St. Paul's. He realized he was seeing St. Paul's Cathedral in London. And in all the images the sun was at its zenith, so the time must be around noon. He'd also been told St. Paul's was a meeting place, so what better location for Leah and himself to meet. He had seen it, but only from a distance as the carriage passed, so he sent his own fleeting impression of the place as if in reassurance that the message had been received. He still had half an idea that he was deluding himself. There was only one way to find out. He must arrange with the Dees for a carriage to take him to London immediately. There was just time to arrive before noon.

Kelley sat at Dr. Dee's writing desk, also deep in concentration, as he struggled to compose a letter to Burghley and Walsingham. He had been practically illiterate when he first came here, but Dee had been insistent about him learning his letters. He still had problems with spelling. The letter read, more or less legibly:

> I have discoverd some information that may be very
> important as regards Her Majesty's safety and welfaire,
> but must conferr with you in pryvate. I will be coming
> to London tomorrow and hope that you will meet with
> me. Relying upon your wise judgement in this matter,
> I remain . . .

Remembering the vividness of the dream in which he'd dispatched Scorpio, he began to tremble, and his shaking hand made a blot on the page. Damn. My life's been a shambles ever since those two showed up. And there's more to that Scorpio than meets the eye, even though what does meet the eye is ugly enough. Him with that stupid mask, and the Queen always teasing at him to remove it in her presence. If I can ever get him to do so, she'll probably fall over in a dead faint.

With the crowds of London at a fever pitch about witches in their midst, the Queen would dare not protect him once he was shown to be a sorcerer.

Dr. Dee appeared in the doorway. "Where have you been? I've been looking all over for you. I'm busy with my astrological calculations, and farmer Rolfe has arrived to consult about his lost cow. I told him you'd be right with him."

Kelley cursed under his breath. Since finances were so straitened, Dee had been taking in money any way he could, even to locating lost articles for the common folk—a cloak, a sack of grain and now even a lost cow. Dr. Dee usually managed to be conveniently busy on these occasions, and Kelley had to use the glass alone.

Grumbling, he went to the séance room. Farmer Rolfe was a great, oafish lout of a man with sun-reddened face who looked and smelled as if he'd come directly from the barnyard.

"The last time I seen her was in the south pasture. We're in sore need without a cow to give milk, so I hope you can help us," said Rolfe as Kelley gritted his teeth and took his place behind the glass.

On such occasions he set aside all the usual flummery that was reserved for richer clients. Simply keeping the room dark was enough to properly awe the countryfolk, who were superstitious to begin with, anyway.

Kelley's eyes inadvertently went to the glass, and he thought he saw shifting patterns of light within it. He averted his eyes slightly and began to work up a proper trance state. The whole thing could be done in a few minutes if he worked it right. He began to spout gibberish in a sonorous voice, noting with satisfaction that Rolfe looked terrified. When I go out on my own, thought Kelley, I'll have an assistant to handle these commonplace matters.

The gibberish suddenly stuck in his throat as he saw curved reflections dancing on the wall before him. Light shimmered like a giant golden bubble, and two figures were taking shape inside it. It's happening, thought Kelley in a panic, what I always feared. Without knowing it, I've called something. He sat paralyzed in the chair as the apparitions came clearer, two man shapes, one broad and muscular, the other thinner with a regal bearing. Both had hideous, bird-like faces, and black robes flapped about their bodies where there should have been no wind blowing. Their red skin and coiling black horns made them look suspiciously like devils. The slender one carried a glowing, golden orb.

Rolfe had been growing more fidgety all the time, and now he couldn't seem to keep himself from throwing a glance over his shoulder where Kelley was staring so fixedly. He looked from the shapes back at Kelley with a new awe.

The figures ballooned large for an instant, then came into reality with an almost audible snap.

"Are they going to help look for my cow?" asked Rolfe innocently as Kelley cowered back from the visitants.

"You fool, they're not part of the show. I don't know where they came from."

This was too much for farmer Rolfe; with a half-suppressed scream he bolted for the door and was gone.

Kelley would have liked to run, too, but the apparitions were between himself and the door. "Avaunt, begone, spirits, I command thee!" he shouted with more conviction than he felt. The two only continued to look at him curiously. He had a sinking feeling that he should have bothered about a magic circle this time.

Ignoring Kelley, the two visitors walked around the séance room, inspecting everything carefully. They were most

interested in the crystal, looking into it and seeing their
weird faces appear even more distorted, and making noises
that sounded to him like evil laughter.

"I conjure thee in the name of—" Kelley began again.

"Silence, worm," said the thinner one. "We seek Scorpio. What can you tell us of him? Lie and I'll move you
around a dimensional corner and turn you inside out. You'll
be able to look down and see the beating of your own heart."

He prostrated himself, babbling almost incoherently.
"Scorpio. He was here, but he went to London for some
purpose. I don't know why. St. Paul's, he said. That is all
I know, your lordships, your Graces, Your Worships. Please
do not harm me!" Being turned inside out didn't sound like
an impossible threat coming from these two.

Seeming to laugh again at Kelley's fear, the spirits
grasped the orb between them and it emitted a burst of light.
Concentric rings of radiance blinded Kelley for the moment,
and when he looked again, they were gone.

Dr. Dee was working busily in his study when Kelley
came bursting in, wild-eyed. "I quit," he said. "I quit your
employ as of now."

"Calm down, man, what's the matter?"

"You kept pushing me into contacting the spirits. Angels,
you said. Don't tell me the things I just saw were angels.
They were red and had horns; tails, too, I think. Yes, definitely tails. They were carrying a golden orb, and—"

It just now occurred to him where he had seen a glowing
sphere like that before, and he also now reflected that there
was something similar between the faces of the apparitions
and that of Scorpio.

"Scorpio," he said. "I never thought to see another face
as misshapen as his. They were looking for him, and they
had an orb, too. He's real, not a fake. A real sorcerer! I
killed him, you know. Yes, I held him underwater until he

stopped breathing. All the time he was only laughing at me, playing with me.''

''Calm yourself, man, you look ready for a fit of apoplexy.''

A real sorcerer, thought Kelley. And all the time, I accused him of being a charlatan. I wonder what awful plans he has for the Queen and the realm. Now it's more important than ever that I unmask him and turn him over to the authorities. Those speaking out against witches are right; there *are* unnatural things about. Once I tell the constable what I know, Scorpio's certain to be imprisoned, maybe even burned as a witch, and then my troubles with him will be over.

Chapter
16

*T*he sun stood just at noon, wreathed in a veil of cloud, as Leah made her way to the cathedral. For all she knew, this was just a fool's errand. It seemed impossible to send messages through the air. But maybe Bothwell had delivered the message for her; there was still a chance that Scorpio had received it that way. It didn't really matter, as long as the result was the same.

She lingered in the nave for a few minutes, and then when no one appeared, she began to walk around the grounds. St. Paul's was a large place. He could be here and she could miss him. No, it would be better to stay in one spot. She stopped by an ornamental fountain.

A moment later she saw Scorpio running toward her.

Leah ran to meet him, and then they both stopped, looking at each other somewhat embarrassedly. Then on impulse Leah reached out and enfolded Scorpio in a hug, oblivious of those who stared at his odd appearance.

"I didn't think it would work. It couldn't work, and yet . . . " stammered Scorpio, looking embarrassed again as Leah released him, as if he were uncertain how to react to her gesture.

"We read each other's thoughts," said Leah. "I seem to remember something about that." She strove to recall what had happened in that dream womb so long ago, but it was no use.

155

"Perhaps this means that we can control the orb with the power of our minds, as Dr. Dee told me," said Scorpio. "Do you know what that would mean?"

"It would mean we'd have our pick of all time and space. We could go anywhere, anywhen."

"We could go back to before your father first became involved with de Signac's intrigues," said Scorpio. "Or better yet, even before you met me."

"I don't know if I'd want that."

"You could have your life back."

"It wouldn't really be my life anymore. Not after all this. I'd surely spend my days waiting for the appearance of a troublesome demon that never arrived."

"Well, you wouldn't have to go back. How about forward? Live in the time that pleases you best."

"It sounds tempting. Then you could go back to your own world."

She supposed she didn't understand what it must be like to be in the midst of folk who were so alien. Terrapin was the only place for him, but still Leah felt almost bereft when she thought of going on to an unknown future without him. Foolish, she thought, to think he could have the same feelings as a human being.

"Anyway, the reason I asked you to meet me here was to warn you about Edward Kelley," she said. "He doesn't just want to steal the orb; he wants you out of the way."

"Thanks for the warning," said Scorpio, "but I'm afraid he's already done his worst."

"Has he actually made an attempt on your life?"

"Better than that, he killed me," said Scorpio with a burble of laughter. He shared the story with Leah, who didn't seem to find it all that humorous.

"I shouldn't have left you there. What if he'd tried something that didn't involve water?"

"I never thought of that," said Scorpio. "But now he won't get the chance."

"I'll have some stories to tell you when there's more time. Anyway, I think I've got Jacob Auerman almost convinced to show us his mysterious talisman. It might still be of help."

"Yes, while I was playing at sorcerer with Dr. Dee, you've been working hard."

"I'll take you to him now."

As they walked by the podium, Leah noticed that the pale, thin speaker was there again, loudly exhorting a knot of interested passersby about the imminent dangers of witchcraft. "Let's hurry; there was almost a riot here earlier," she said.

As the man stood there, gesticulating wildly, behind him a vision began to form, within expanding rings of golden light. His audience, some of whom had been heckling him, suddenly became riveted, and the speaker waxed even more eloquent.

Leah and Scorpio stood frozen in fear as the apparitions grew more solid and recognizable. "Hunters! Here!" said Leah. "I thought we had lost them centuries ago."

"Run, hide!" shouted Scorpio, for once letting his instincts have full sway. They both turned to run, but the crowd began to scream and panic as they became aware of the alien visitors, jostling and pushing Scorpio and Leah and giving them no room to run.

Ardon, the larger of the two Hunters, put out a hand and grabbed the skinny speaker around the neck, lifting him straight up off the ground and cutting his discourse short. Then he tossed the man aside as easily as if he were a bag of meal and pointed toward Scorpio. "Lethor, there he is! Let's get him!"

A voice cut through the noise. "There, that deformed man is the sorcerer." Leah saw Kelley alight from a carriage and run toward them. "He's the demon-conjuror. And the woman is his apprentice. Seize them or all is lost!"

The crowd rallied, their attention still divided. A pot-bellied merchant looked as if he were about to lay hands on Scorpio, who tossed back the cowl of his robe. Seeing this alien visage, the merchant and those standing nearby recoiled, leaving an avenue of escape.

Leah and Scorpio wasted no time taking advantage of this; they began to run.

"Don't be afraid. He can't resist all of you," shouted Kelley. The mob took his words to heart and gave chase.

The two Hunters also tried to follow, but they were effectively cut off from their prey by a ravening mob. Ardon drew his laser and looked as if he were about to cut his way through the crowd, but Lethor gestured for him to put it away. "There are too many of them for that to be effective," he said. Hunter ethics prevented gratuitous slaughter. Killing was always done with a purpose in mind.

"This way," panted Leah, pushing Scorpio toward the cathedral and sparing a look over her shoulder to see how close the front runners of the mob had come. She judged that they were still far enough ahead for what she had in mind.

"We can never outrun them," gasped Scorpio.

"We don't have to. I learned a little something while I was gone."

She remembered Lord Foistwell holding forth about knowing every nook and cranny of a place before planning a crime there. She didn't really know every detail about St. Paul's, since it was such a large place, but she thought she remembered something that would be helpful. There had been ongoing attempts at repair of the crumbling old building, and she had earlier noticed where a loose wooden panel in the wall had been put back carelessly. There was only a very small space behind it. She hoped that both she and

Scorpio would fit. There was little time to try it for size; they crammed themselves into the musty crevice, and Leah let the panel fall back over them.

They heard the thunder of the crowd's feet as they dashed by, shouting, "Death to the witches. This way, I can hear their footsteps!"

"We must wait until we're sure they have gone," whispered Leah. The cramped space gave her a claustrophobic feeling, and if the sharp eyes of the Hunters should notice that this section of the paneling didn't quite fit together— She shivered, remembering previous experiences with the alien beings.

Time passed and the dark, cramped quarters began to remind her of the dream womb inside the orb where both their minds had been linked. The telepathy that had brought them to St. Paul's was a poor thing compared to it, but she realized that that was where the link had originated. More orb travel would no doubt accentuate it. She wondered whether it was a good idea for beings so different to share such a close communion. They had already decided they were bound for separate futures, once their problems with the orb and the Hunters were resolved.

When they peered out after a wait of several more minutes, the mob had passed, and there was no sign of the Hunters. No doubt they'd followed the others.

"Lord Foist was right," said Leah. "Now we must make our way to the Jewish quarter."

Chapter
17

*L*eah and Scorpio hurried toward the Jewish quarter, keeping a close eye for any sign of possible pursuers.

"I don't understand," said Scorpio. "You say you enrolled in a thieves' school in order to get the amulet away from Auerman."

"I learned all the lessons quite well," said Leah, "but I failed the final test, which was to actually steal something. I must have been the school's biggest failure."

"But you think you're going to have access to the secret because you *didn't* steal it."

"It seems so."

"This is a confusing world, isn't it?"

"That's a conclusion I have often come to."

Esther Green gave Scorpio a sharp look, but she escorted them to Auerman's study. "You said earlier that if Jacob Auerman had a chance to listen to your story, he might help," said Leah. "I think you were right. I could have tried to explain, but you're the logical one to plead your case."

Auerman greeted them in the study, and this time listened patiently to all that Scorpio had to tell. When he finished his tale, Auerman's expression was rapt. It was as if he had discovered that his ideas about the possibilities of En Sof, the infinite, were even greater than he had imagined.

"About this other world," he said. "I believe you. And to return to save the lives of your people is something I understand. Do you truly think the secret of the symbol will help you master your orb-craft?"

"We have to try," said Leah.

"Yes, I can see that you do." The old Kabbalist bent his head and took the amulet from around his neck. Deliberately, he handed it to Scorpio, as if he feared to let it get out of his possession after all these years.

Leah took it and carefully unrolled the tiny scroll, using the dexterity Lord Foist had taught her.

"I can't read it," said Auerman. "But perhaps you can. It's written in Provençal by an early Kabbalist scholar."

Haltingly, she read the words written in fading sepia ink: "On the Chariot Throne sat a being with two aspects. On the right, the male, on the left, female. Neither could see the other and each was kept from moving by the opposing force of the other. The Matrona, the female, spread out from her place and adhered to the male side until he moved away from his side and she came to unite with him face-to-face. And when they united, they appeared as veritably one body. When they were one, the moon waxed full—" Here Leah paused.

"Or maybe the sphere became complete," she said uncertainly, and then continued. "And the fiery chariot ascended to the realm of dreams."

There was more, on the same order. When Leah had finished reading, she looked at Auerman expectantly. "Do you know what this signifies?"

"There is an ancient Kabbalistic tradition that the Deity has a feminine counterpart, not, as one might think, representing softness and kindness, but rather, stern judgment and demonic power. Her symbol is the moon. It may mean only that a man should keep in touch with the feminine aspect of reality by taking a good wife, but it may mean much more. It is too soon to judge. We must study this further to see what it might mean. Can you come tomorrow?''

"I'm sorry," said Scorpio, "but our time here grows short."

Thanking Auerman, they left and paused outside, deciding what to do next. "Do you think anything we learned will prove useful?" asked Leah. "It talked of a cooperation between the male and the female. We are male and female."

"Yes, but that should mean that we can master the orb, but that the Hunters cannot. That's the exact opposite of how it is."

"There was mention of a glowing orb."

"Or only the moon," said Scorpio. "I'm afraid it was too arcane to give us any help with our present problem."

"Your experiments with mind control of the orb are promising, but there's so much we don't know," said Leah. "We may have to consider any possible clue, even the most obscure. We simply have to keep trying until we master it."

"The mobs here make me nervous," said Scorpio. "Maybe we'd best return to Mortlake. The Dees' carriage is still waiting at Whitehall."

"That's a good idea, but perhaps we should travel separately. Someone might spot us and remember that we were together at the cathedral. It will also give the Hunters two different trails to follow. It could confuse them."

"All right," said Scorpio, "I'll meet you back at Mortlake, but be careful."

Chapter
18

*A*rdon picked his way down a street littered with disgusting substances, wondering what sort of people could live in these hovels. Above, clouds were gathering and beginning to rumble with thunder. Ardon muttered to himself about the uncomfortable tightness of his skin in this high humidity. If it began to rain, they would have to duck under a roof quickly before the moisture made their hides blister and crack. Both Hunters bore the scars of being drenched while chasing Scorpio in Avignon. Hopefully, the rain would hold off until they'd done this little job.

Ardon lifted his hand in signal to Lethor to show that he had checked out this side of the street and had seen nothing of the Aquay or the girl. That was like an Aquay, he thought, dragging a native into what should have been kept private. But since the female had chosen to play a role in this, she would have to take what came. She could certainly expect no mercy from him; that was the rule the Hunters always played by, and they were scrupulous about their own rules.

Having their orb to bear them to different locations didn't help because this city was a maze of dirty streets, and the only way to find their prey now was to search every one in the general vicinity.

They moved on down the street, store owners slamming closed their shutters at sight of them, passersby tending to

pass by on the opposite side of the thoroughfare. They would
have captured them at the cathedral if that earless rogue had
not interfered. Ardon's hatred was slow and methodical,
like all of his emotions. As he lumbered along, he considered the ways and means of Kelley's death for a long time.
That was pleasant. But he saw that Lethor was signaling to
him to enter the next street. Lethor liked to do things fast,
and it was sometimes hard to figure out what he wanted.

Ahead of him in the narrow, winding street, he saw a
familiar figure; he homed his near-vision in on her to make
sure. It was she, the girl Leah. He raised his hand and
waved it in the prearranged gesture that meant the prey had
been identified. Of course, it would have been much easier
for the two of them to slink up behind her and drill a hole
in her back with laserfire, but tradition said a Hunter had
to let his victim see him first. The hunt became more exciting
that way. Ardon began to feel excited, despite his phleg-
matic disposition.

He saw Lethor dart back behind the buildings, evidently
trying to get ahead of her. Sure enough, he saw his lean
companion leap from the shadow of one of the shops, and
it was obvious the prey had seen him, because she began
to run in earnest. It didn't matter, thought Ardon, because
the Hunters would always run faster.

Leah felt clumsy and foolish as the Hunter appeared so
nonchalantly before her, as if he'd been tracking her all this
time without her knowing it. This was the warning Scorpio
had talked about, Hunter etiquette. She stood in front of a
barbershop. The white pole with its red striping, indicative
that the barber also bled people as a cure for illness, seemed
a ghastly symbol under the circumstances. She knew that
there were two of them, but she didn't see the other. Perhaps, like she and Scorpio, they had decided to split their
forces to cover more ground. She could only hope so. The

Hunter was larger and stronger than she was and could outrun and outjump her. The only advantage she might possibly have was that she'd worked this neighborhood as a thief, and she knew the terrain. Perhaps the alien did not. She scanned the sky. Perhaps it was too much to hope that a downpour would make the aliens seek shelter.

She ran with all her might, ducking into alleys, crawling under broken foundations, dodging past oncoming traffic, her terror making her reckless. Daring a look over her shoulder, she could not see a pursuer. Possibly, her strategies had worked. Her spirits fell when she caught a glimpse of another silhouette at a corner. He moved back, to hide behind a pile of crates, but he didn't move fast enough to escape detection. Seeing him forced her to move off in an unplanned direction. She had the panicked feeling that the two of them were herding her to a place she didn't wish to go.

She was sure of this later when she reached the mouth of an alleyway and darted inside, the stink of corruption rising around her. In the semidarkness she heard scuttling noises and saw a rat's naked tail slip behind a pile of debris. She was so aware of the real threat behind her that nothing so familiar as a rat could frighten her now.

From the positions of the two pursuers behind her, the alley was the only place she had left to go. It appeared to be a blind alley from the street, but previous experience with this quarter told her that between a building and a mound of rubble was a small egress, wide enough for a small person to squeeze through. She didn't think she'd be able to do it with them so close on her trail, though. She needed time to make her escape, a distraction—anything.

She heard the inexorable *pad-pad-pad* of the Hunters' feet on the cobbles and realized they were closer than she had thought. As her hand brushed the pouch at her side, she felt something angular through the cloth. She'd forgotten about this. Maybe it would work. At this point she had to try.

Ardon was beginning to feel a little fatigue from the long chase. This female was stronger than she looked, and she had been good prey. Ardon hoped that Lethor would give her the honor of dying with a clean shot between the eyes, rather than drawing it out, as he sometimes did, for fun. Obviously, this stench-filled corridor between structures was closed at one end by a slide of rubble, so now that she was in, she was trapped. All that was left to do was for Lethor to go in and make the kill. It was dark inside, but the prey was surely not dangerous. Ardon wondered why his companion was hesitating.

"I hear something," said Lethor. "She can't escape, perhaps she's coming this way."

"Do you hear her footsteps?"

"I hear something, some odd noise. But she is the only one who went in there and the only one who could be stirring."

"Except possibly vermin."

"Other vermin," said Lethor, and they shared a laugh. Who ever said Hunters didn't have a good sense of humor? Ardon wondered. Now he could hear the sound, too. Something was coming this way, but it was an odd, buzzing, clicking sort of sound.

It was coming closer. Both of them tensed, fingers on the studs of their weapons.

A mannikin made of metal whirred and clicked as it walked shakily down the alleyway's cobblestone surface. Lethor's curse was loud in the confined space. He turned his laser on the toy and incinerated it and then dashed into the alley. Ardon heard him curse again and ran in, to see Lethor staring at a very small escape hatch through the pile of rubble.

"She looked too tired to get far," said Lethor hopefully.

Then both of them looked up as they heard raindrops begin to patter in the streets outside. "Take cover," screamed Ardon as an errant raindrop touched his skin with a sizzling sound.

Chapter
19

*S*corpio made his way back to where he'd left Dr. Dee's carriage and hastened toward it. A slight shower had washed the streets, leaving them glistening, but now the clouds were clearing away. He hoped Leah was safe. He should have insisted she come back with him and ride to Mortlake in the carriage, but at the moment it had seemed like a good idea to split up to confuse the Hunters.

He was about to greet the driver when he saw that the carriage was occupied. Edward Kelley sat with a stout, muscular man in some sort of official-looking uniform with an emblem on it. Two others, armed guardsmen, sat opposite them. Scorpio didn't think he liked the look of things. It appeared to be a trap.

In the confusion of the moment, he retreated, but found himself approaching the palace. He still carried the mask he had worn, in a fold of his robe, so he stopped and donned it. He approached the guards at the front gate, holding out his hand to show the signet ring the Queen had given him as a token. "You know this seal," he said. "Her Majesty has summoned me on a matter of great import."

The guards, seeing Elizabeth's seal on the ring, let him pass.

Hide! Flee! his instincts were telling him, but he knew the palace was large, and there would surely be a spot he could hide in until Kelley gave up his search.

"Scorpio," said a voice. He looked up to see a woman dressed like a fairy princess, with a sparkling mask and frail wings of gauze attached at either shoulder. He thought he recognized her as one of the ladies of the Privy Chamber, though he didn't know them all by name.

"The Queen was not expecting you."

"I was not expecting myself," he said, which made the lady laugh.

"We're preparing for a masked ball this evening. Why not attend? You're already dressed for it."

"Well, I don't—I'm not—" he began, but the lady soon had him in tow, chattering at him animatedly. He was always at a loss on human social occasions, but perhaps his luck was not entirely bad. Surely, Kelley's search could not include the Queen's hall in the midst of a gala celebration.

He heard lively music playing from behind huge double doors, and as he entered, he felt in the midst of chaos. It was as if this were a convocation of worlds, and each one had sent as a representative its most bizarre and colorful species. Velvets, spangles, and cloth of gold had been used in lavish display. Outlandish masks covered the faces of the guests, and for the first time since he'd been here, he felt inconspicuous.

Tables, running the length of the hall, offered a vast selection of wines and dainties, so he lingered here, nibbling this or that morsel, hoping to lie low until Kelley gave up.

A man dressed in Roman toga with a silver mask of comedy held before his face jostled Scorpio at the banquet table. Though these were courtiers, Scorpio noticed that their behavior was uninhibited. They drank and danced unrestrainedly and were likely to play coarse practical jokes or indulge in rude jests.

"Did you hear the latest? Musicians are healthy because they live by good airs," said the man, slapping Scorpio on the back and laughing loudly. "D'you get it, music . . . airs?"

Though he tried to squirm away, the man continued. "Did you know a cannibal is the lovingest man to his enemy, for willingly no man eats what he loves not."

After a few more of these *bons mots,* Scorpio was able to excuse himself and escape from the jokester.

Kelley was arguing loudly with the guardsmen at the gate just as Walsingham's carriage arrived. "What's this all about?" Walsingham asked, recognizing Kelley as Dee's assistant.

"This lout allowed a dangerous sorcerer to pass the gates, and for all I know he's gone to work his evil magics on the Queen herself."

"A threat against the Queen—" began Walsingham, his protective instincts aroused. "Who is the scoundrel?"

"You know him as Scorpio of the Aquay, and I believe he's managed to worm his way into Her Majesty's good graces, but I've come into possession of some interesting information concerning the invoking of demons."

"I never cared for that mask and that shrilling voice," said Walsingham. "I should have known there was something amiss about him. You say he's gone to harm the Queen?"

"Yes, and I've brought the law with me to deal with the beggar," said Kelley, gesturing toward the constable and three guardsmen who had accompanied him. "But these fools have let him enter."

"He had the Queen's seal," said the gateman. "How was I to know?"

"Let us in and we'll apprehend the felon," said the constable self-importantly.

"Do you realize the court is holding a masked ball this evening?" demanded Walsingham. "I don't approve of

such mummery, of course, but the Queen loves her enter-
tainments. But, see here, I can't let you go barging in among
the guests. It would cause a scandal.''

"We must uphold the law," said the constable.

"Then you must do it in costume," said Walsingham,
"and you must cause no disturbance. If you search and find
that Scorpio isn't there, you must go away quietly."

"All right," said Kelley, "but I'm sure he'll be there."

Once inside, Walsingham sent a servant to fetch costumes
for Kelley and his men. Grumblingly, they put them on.
Kelley was given a jester's motley, and bells jingled at every
step as he approached the hall. Now I'll have my revenge
on the boggart, he thought. Walking closely together, they
strolled among the guests. "Remember that this is the
Queen's hall," he whispered to the others. "We can have
no disturbance here or it may be our heads."

"Are you enjoying yourself, Scorpio?" asked the lady
who had conducted him here.

"Yes, very much," he said.

"I think the costumes are so very exciting," she said.
"Some are quite grotesque. You should have seen the pair
in black robes and skullcaps. I don't know how they did it,
but they'd varnished their skin a brilliant red. And those
ram's horns on their heads—"

"Where? Where did you see them?" asked Scorpio, suddenly feeling panic. A crowd of bizarrely dressed folk that
could hide *him* could hide others as well. "If you see them
again, don't go near them," he said. "I'm afraid I must go
now."

"But you haven't yet danced."

"I'm ignorant of such a human custom, my lady."

The orchestra struck up a pavane.

"It's easy to learn. I could teach you."

Scorpio was about to take flight when he realized that the

man in the jester costume was approaching him rapidly, and he didn't look friendly. In fact, a closer look at him revealed Kelley's general build and swaggering walk. The lady was pulling him toward the line of dancers, so he let himself be towed there and tried to mimic her motions.

It was no use. He, who was as graceful as a shark in water, was totally at a loss on a dance floor. Some of the other dancers got out of his way; others stopped to laugh at him. His face was hot with shame until he realized the room had gone silent and someone was standing before him.

Her head was hidden in a casque set with black brilliants, from which rose tall, feathery antennae. A black domino obscured her eyes. Behind her head was an enormous lace collar in the fanciful shape of a butterfly, sprinkled with sparkling, varicolored gems. Her immense, flaring skirt was yellow with black butterfly markings.

Those around her were bowing, but he would have known her anyway by the long-fingered white hand she held out to him. She signaled the orchestra to play on, and in the midst of the costumed court, Elizabeth asked him to dance. "I couldn't, Your Majesty," he said. "With my clumsiness I'll make a spectacle of us both."

"That's the beauty of being a queen," she said. "I can make a spectacle of myself whenever I wish, and no one *dares* laugh."

"I thank you, Your Majesty," said Scorpio when the dance ended. "I feel very honored, but I really must go. It would be better for everyone concerned."

Before he had a chance to leave, Kelley jingled up to him, flanked by the men of the law. "Pardon us, your ladyship," said Kelley, who had evidently not recognized the Queen, "but you don't know who you were dancing with. He is an evil sorcerer, master of the black arts. I personally have seen the devils he conjured forth."

"You think I'm a charlatan like yourself," said Scorpio,

"because you trick the gullible out of a few coins with your so-called talent of scrying."

"So-called," sputtered Kelley. "I'll have you know that I've been very successful in calling up the spirits by means of a crystal. My contacts, Madimi and Medicina, have imparted to me many arcane secrets, which Dr. Dee writes in his book."

The constable began to eye Kelley as he bragged of his prowess with the showstone. "I think the authorities would also be interested in one who calls up the spirits," he said. "Surely, this, too, is unnatural."

"No, no, you misunderstand. It is angels I speak with . . . angels."

"You call them angels. Well, we can sort all that out at Newgate Prison," said the constable. "Scorpio of Aquay, I arrest you in the name of—"

"The name of the Queen?" said Elizabeth, lowering her domino so they could see to whom they spoke.

"Begging your pardon, Your . . . Your Majesty," said Kelley, doffing his belled cap.

Though the others were riveted by fear, a long-standing grudge made Kelley sidle toward Scorpio. When he was close enough, he reached up and plucked the mask from the being's face.

Several ladies standing nearby screamed when Scorpio was unmasked. And the Queen looked shocked at first.

"There, you see, unmasked as a conjuror," said Kelley. "Can you not see it by his face?"

"It is as I had once guessed," said Elizabeth softly. "A handsome countenance. Though, I'll admit, very different than how I had imagined it. I think you told the truth when you said you came from a world far from here."

She spoke more sternly. "Would anyone dare to interrupt *my* festivities, to threaten *my* honored guests?" And the guardsmen retreated, leaving Kelley alone with Elizabeth's wrath.

The answer to the Queen's question seemed to be yes, because at that moment Scorpio saw two tall, black-draped figures cross the room and focus their weapons on him.

He whirled around and began to run, hoping to draw them away from the Queen and her courtiers. A flash of laserfire sizzled along a tabletop beside him, turning every dish to flambé as he took to his heels. A glance over his shoulder showed him that two of the Queen's gentlemen-pensioners had advanced to protect her, drawing their swords.

He saw a laser burst hit a sword blade, and the poor guardsman watched as his steel bowed, melted and puddled on the floor. Then Scorpio saw no more as he darted from the room.

Chapter
20

*L*eah, having hitched a ride with a farmer on his dray, arrived at Mortlake, expecting to find Scorpio there. When she didn't see him, she couldn't hide her concern from Dr. Dee.

"Something's wrong, isn't it?" he said. "I should have known it when Edward came in here like a man demented, offering to quit my service and babbling that the angels we summoned were really devils."

"That means the Hunters have been here," said Leah.

"Can you explain any of this to me?"

"Only that the Hunters are aliens like Scorpio, and they want to kill us." She explained to him how his clockwork mannikin had diverted the Hunters' attention long enough for her to escape, and Dr. Dee laughed at the idea of the savage aliens waiting at the mouth of the alley for one of his toys to walk out. "I thought it was clever to come here by different routes, but maybe we should have stayed together. It's getting late. Maybe they've already found him."

"You're going to go, aren't you?" said Dee.

"We have to, if it isn't already too late." Leah paced the room, waiting, as night fell.

At last a dispirited-looking Scorpio entered, having come most of the way on foot.

"I thought they'd caught you," said Leah. This time she held back from embracing him. It wouldn't do to embarrass him with her human concern for his welfare. She couldn't help feeling it, though, however much it was wasted.

"They did, but they lost me again," he said in an exhausted voice. "I hope we'll be safe here, at least for a little while."

"We won't be safe," said Leah. "They've already been here, looking for us. Kelley saw them. When they can't find us in London, they'll surely think of Mortlake. We have to get the orb and jump again."

Scorpio covered his face with his hands. "They have an orb, too. No matter where we go in time and space, they'll seek us out. I don't know why I thought I could make a difference all by myself; none of my people would have thought of such a thing, except maybe Leandro," he amended softly.

"You're not by yourself," said Leah. "You have me."

"And me," added Dr. Dee.

"That's the problem, don't you understand? I've turned your lives upside down, moving in times and places I have no business in. I have no right to bring my problems into your lives or to cause you to care about them."

"Don't say that," said Dr. Dee. "Mankind must continue to discover, and explore, whether it be in time and space or in the realm of ideas."

"And so must womankind," said Leah.

Scorpio looked up. "The scroll," he said. "The way your society is set up, the natural assumption is that men think with logic and women by intuition, but what if it wasn't talking about male and female at all? What if that was only a metaphor for the two aspects of the mind: the side that plods along, putting one fact together with another, and the side that makes wild intuitive leaps of the imagination? Could my problem with controlling the orb be that I'm trying too hard for control?"

"At the primordial point, all opposites must be understood as potentially present," said Dee thoughtfully. "You might be able to balance your mind between logic and dream. A worthy theory, but theories need proving."

"We don't have any time for proving theories," said Leah.

The sudden rattling of the door latch startled them.

"The Hunters!" said Leah. "Who else could it be? A locked door won't keep them out for long."

Dee opened one of the windows. "Make your exit this way. I'll try to delay them a few moments."

"Don't put yourself in danger," said Scorpio. "They're deadly assassins."

"Don't you see, I want to find out what they're like, even though they might be dangerous."

"Thank you, Dr. Dee," said Scorpio as Leah frantically pushed him toward the window. They tumbled into the wet grass below and began to run toward the stagnant lake. Scorpio sent out a tendril of thought and plunged it deep into the water. A ray of light, like a beacon, shot skyward from the orb hidden on the murky bottom, guiding them.

Scorpio tried to ignore the two looming silhouettes that paced them from behind, but they became impossible to ignore as a laser burst arced into the grass beside him with a hissing sound. Another shot sped past so close to Leah that it caught her skirt on fire. He heard her scream, saw her slap at the flames.

"That's all right," he told her. "We're close enough. Grab me and hold on tight."

Scorpio felt her fingers dig into his rib cage, and he leapt. He heard the fire go out with a sizzle. Water closed around him, feeling heavy and smothering at first, then giving way to the buoyancy and freedom he always felt in the water.

He swam strongly. The Hunters wouldn't dive because of the damage it would do to their skins.

Following his tendril of thought, Scorpio went unerringly

to where the orb lay half buried in mud and slime. Leah let go her hold with one hand, and the water made her swirl around him as if they danced. A moment later they held the orb between them, and Scorpio could feel the mind connection, like a three-way link, solid, reassuring. Neither of them could stay down here indefinitely without surfacing, though he could stay longer. But it didn't matter; the Hunters waited above, and there was only one way out.

Jump, said Leah's mind.

Jump, came the echo from his own.

And the future waited.